SOJOURNER

in

Walnut Creek, San Francisco,
Paris, Florence, Amsterdam,
Lubbock, Toronto, Brooklyn, and Manhattan.

Florence, Naples, Rome, Venice,
S. Francesco, Orvieto, Volterra,
Assisi, and Poznan.

By Lee Foust

Copyright © 2012 by Lee Foust

ISBN 978-0-7414-8117-7 Paperback
ISBN 978-0-7414-8118-4 Hardcover
ISBN 978-0-7414-8119-1 eBook
Library of Congress Control Number: 2012919933

Printed in the United States of America

This is a work of fiction. Names, characters, places, and incidents either are the product of the author's imagination or are used fictitiously. Any resemblance to actual events or locales or persons, living or dead, is entirely coincidental.

Published January 2013

INFINITY PUBLISHING
1094 New DeHaven Street, Suite 100
West Conshohocken, PA 19428-2713
Toll-free (877) BUY BOOK
Local Phone (610) 941-9999
Fax (610) 941-9959
Info@buybooksontheweb.com
www.buybooksontheweb.com

This book goes out to my other mother,

Gretchen Dumont Blair Hughes,

who made it possible in so many ways,

with much appreciation and love.

CONTENTS

I dreamed I lay in an opium den in the Mission District
of San Francisco last night, drinking a bottle of scotch.
I fell asleep and was awakened
by a belligerent gang of teenagers spoiling for a fight.
Instead of fighting
I threw a roll of sourdough bread
out onto Valencia Street.
An ugly water glass fell over and smashed
all of my delicate and beautiful champagne
and martini glasses.
Then I had to pay up and go home.

DEEP IN THE HOUSES (a song of sorts)

Deep in the houses
lost in the suburbs
porcelain fear, porcelain terror
teenage killers of lovesick parents

Out of the houses
into machine-wrecks
beer in the right hand, line in the left
teenage lovers in still-life car stops

Into the streetlights
America soul-less
another lost gesture, another enclosure
teenage murder in lovesick suburbs
teenage trauma in still-life mug shots

In the shadows I find
slow movement to pass
walking the strip-lights
it's come to the end, love
it's the end of this feeling
I saw a man inside there
pray to his god, love
nothing was seen then
nothing would open
it's come to the end, love
it's the end of this feeling

I saw a man inside there
pray to his god, love
nothing was seen then
nothing would open
it's come to the end, love

1981
Walnut Creek, CA

HOUSE HUNTING

The first thing you need to do is case the neighborhood; check out all of the streets in the area, walk around between the buildings, and imagine yourself passing by these places every day. You have to be lucky too. You have to imagine yourself coming home to it, wanting to go back, night after night, yours for better or worse. You don't want to be driven out sooner than you feel like going. You have to be prepared for what the place might do to you, how it might make you feel. You have to love it a little before so you don't hate it later.

The place I was looking at that day was down South of Market, in the industrial part of town—which is kind of schizophrenic too, having little bits of the other parts of the city in it as well. I was walking around and under the freeway that skims above the cross streets—it's too low down here to have any buildings sitting up under it—and then arches up to become the Bay Bridge further down over the even-numbered piers this side of the ferry building. I was checking out the topography of the neighborhood, its low warehouses and typical San Francisco-style three-floor Victorian flats, the old established wholesale businesses leaning up close to the sidewalks, ambitious new factory outlet distributors sitting back behind renovated art deco façades and minimalist parking lots, a few grimy liquor store/corner markets, and the occasional deli for the local employees to lunch at.

Of course the bars: the anonymous final resting places of derelict alcoholics on Fifth Street between the dirty magazine newsstands, the pawn shops, barred liquor stores, and boarded-up storefronts, or the scattered gay and lesbian nightclubs fanning out toward the Mission, hip and cliquey: the disco-pounding Stud, nude dancing Clementina's, or the leather bikers' enormous S.F. Eagle. The Eagle had a sign out that day, "Slave auction tonight!" These underground spots would pave the way for what was to become the club-going center of San Francisco in the late eighties but, on the day that I'm talking about, there was only the silly disco with the swimming pool, the Oasis, and the brand-new hip post-punk art-school restaurant, the Billboard Café. Above all this low-level and rather nondescript warehouse-styled area poked the one edifice in the whole neighborhood that could challenge the freeway for height, the pink stucco church at Tenth and Howard. The shrine next to it, behind the cyclone fence and the well-groomed lawn, with the Madonna and child nestled in a plaster of paris cave, also pink, always reminded me of the eighteenth hole in a miniature golf course.

I decided, that day, that I really liked the South of Market and that I *did* want to live there. It's one of the real parts of the city, a whole landscape that just happened over time and completely by accident. Other parts of San Francisco have been made, claimed, and then cultivated by one demographic or another, like the Haight or the Castro, but nobody had ever cared enough about the South of Market or the Mission or even downtown really to ever make them over completely.

I walked along, looking closely at everything and really thinking about the area for the first time, trying to imagine myself living there through the summer, the fall, and the rainy winter—I was wondering how it would change. In my baggy pants and overcoat, the fog and the old buildings, wet and gray, around me, I remember it like a film noir from the '40s. I probably looked a little like Sterling Hayden, all tall and loose as I am, or maybe, being alone and eyeing everything so suspiciously, I was coming off more determined, like a desperate Richard Widmark character. Inside myself, though, I was feeling cool and glib, like my hero Robert Mitchum. The wind was cold, and it made me walk faster after a while, although I knew that it would eventually blow the fog away—thinking that was already cheering me up. I pushed my hands against the seams of my thrift store overcoat's pockets and felt myself grinning excitedly as I found the little alleyway where my appointment was to be. It was beautiful and tragic, quaint and decaying; it dead-ended underneath the freeway in a parking lot cul-de-sac, a wash of trash blown into a sagging cyclone fence bordering the uneven blacktop.

Anticipation came down as I counted the numbers of the buildings up to where I would be meeting my prospective housemates. You know, you guess that it's that building up ahead, the one with the great big windows, or that one across the street with the enormous Victorian stoop, Corinthian columns, and ornate woodwork shining behind the only shade tree on the block. Then you're expectant, or disappointed, as the buildings ahead vary from cramped modern cement jobs to well-painted Victorians with high ceilings and bay windows. I mean, style is important; it's the mood that the place puts you in that counts most. I pegged the building toward which I was headed too soon, and I knew its type: a sprawling Victorian apartment house—more long than tall, with lots of small units. It started at the very dead end of the alley but stretched about a third of the way down the block toward Folsom Street. Somebody had painted it yellow.

Once there had been four open-air stairwells, two doors to a floor, two floors to the building, old Western movie boarding-house style, but the stairs had been too secluded, dark, and inviting for the little back alleyway, so the landlord had put big cage-like black metal gates over their entrances at street level. There was a panel of buzzers by each gate. One corresponded to the address that I had in my hand.

I stopped and looked quickly around and decided that this wasn't such a bad block. I liked the randomness of everything down here, the openness. Garbage isn't as conspicuous in wide alleys as in the narrower, tree-lined streets in North Beach or up on Russian Hill. And these backstreets are quiet and cool, didn't scare me like the noisy Tenderloin sometimes did with all of its frenetic resentment and opportunity-seeking stares. Anyway, the grimy air's the same all over the city, even if the black dust maybe settles a little bit thicker on these streets that probably never get cleaned. At least there was a place for the drunks to piss, down at the end of the alley, instead of their having to do it in your doorway like they do in the Tenderloin. It was ugly down there at the end of the street, sterile and blacktopped, looped around by that defeated cyclone fence and some tangled-up barbed wire, nothing growing in the shadow of the freeway. You almost couldn't hear the traffic up above, even though you were right under it. Who knows what goes on down there?

This was, at the time, the up-and-coming part of town too. There were lots of artists' lofts and shit, more moving in all the time; things were happening down here, and if I could get in on the scene just as it was about to explode ... and anyway, it's the last part of the city to get the fog.

I didn't hear anything when I pushed the buzzer — once white, now smudged with greasy black, newsprint fingerprints — so I knew right away that the apartment was up on the second floor. I felt bad about the interview being on a day like this. The lumpy summer fog was still loping by, just overhead, and seemed to be pressing down on the squat buildings. I watched the gray globs moving inland, away from the city, and knew that I liked places a lot less when I saw them on overcast days. But, then again, I'd seen some pretty ugly places look at least cheerful because of a sunny day, so I guess it all evens out in some weird, unfair way. This place was starting to feel bad now, but I was determined to give it an even chance.

There were so many things to be considered all of the sudden, and it was hard, then, to make a lot of firm decisions about the future. I was afraid of doing something really wrong because it seemed to matter more now if I did. It was really like a test of myself somehow, of what I could do alone.

I heard the upstairs door open, the sound of scampering feet coming down the stairs, then a face blinked into view and looked out at me from the shadowy stairwell behind the bars. It was Christ, a typical hippie look: blue eyes against dark skin in a bony face with a beard of sorts. "Twenty-three A?" he asked me, with a Latinate "Ah" sound for the letter A. I nodded, and he said, "Follow me," motioning with a single finger, turning his slightly stooped back on me to climb the stairs. His skinny arms dragged him up the handrails to the second floor. I followed, his loose leather flip-flops slapping in my face as we went up.

The roommate referral service had advertised my prospective housemates as Enrique and Miguel, and I was already having visions of a young Picasso and Juan Gris sharing a South of Market loft: pitchers of Sangria and intense aesthetic conversations lasting 'til dawn, presided over by dark and passionate canvases leaned against the walls. Instead, the film was in color now, unpredictable as a Godard or a Fellini, crazy and mannered, from the early sixties, but definitely pre-Beatles, without irony.

The apartment was a cramped mess. There was some loud and completely uninspired hillbilly rock-and-roll or Claptonesque dreck coming from a department store stereo on the floor of what passed for a living room—really only a wider section of the hall—and, besides the stereo, the room held only an imitation leather recliner and a knee-high stack of old *Playboy* and *Penthouse* magazines. My guide then showed me to my prospective room, which was way too small for my stuff and had only one dirty little window in the corner, letting on to an internal air shaft. Finally, I followed Jesus into the kitchen at the dead end of the hall, and there he picked up where my buzz had interrupted him, making soup using a Styrofoam Cup O' Noodles mix as a base.

I sat down at the table where he was working, chopping and mixing various ingredients. Behind him, two enormous and frail-looking windows let in the flat gray light that came from the now solidly cloud-covered sky. Behind my guide's dark silhouette, the view was vast: a sharp, silvery, bran' spankin' new warehouse and a vacant lot filled with tall reeds and even cattails. I found out later that that lot was the easiest and most frequented spot for shooting heroin down South of Market; that it was San Francisco's own Needle Park.

"I am from Italy," Jesus told me finally. "I am the one moving out, moving up to Oregon." We'd passed one of the roommates in the hallway, as he'd come out of the shower, and I'd introduced myself. His name was Enrique, and the Italian had told me that Enrique ran the household and shared the front room with his brother, Miguel, as the towel-covered figure had gone off to his room, droplets of water caught in the light of the bare bulb in the hallway, looking like a skin disease on his neck and shoulders. Now we were in the kitchen chatting about working and living in the country versus the city, Jesus having much trouble finding the English for what eventually came out as, "I don't see how you can live all the time in the city. Is crazy, crazy." I asked him where he'd grown up, and he'd told me in a "small village," as he chopped up much garlic and onions for his soup. "Real Italian soup," he grinned, enjoying grinning. "You like garlic?"

"Mmm, very much."

"It is, you know," he shook his knife at me, "the oldest antibiotic. Antibiotic, but natural. If you get a, a cut, on your arm," he held out his arm, nodding and gesturing toward it with the knife, "and you rub garlic or onion on it, it will stop the infection. I learn that in India."

"What were you doing in India? Working or traveling?"

"Working? No. Is impossible to work there. Well, possible," (grin), "but … I do some business, but I was there mostly for travel."

He chopped his garlic and onions leaning over, his spine curling under the tank top in his concentration, still wearing bell-bottomed pants that hung too low, a little wooden cross on a loose string of beads dangling in front of us, off of his neck. There was a patch of colored cloth holding the cross to its string of beads.

"Are you from the city?"

"No, not originally. I grew up out in the suburbs, but I've lived here for about two years now." He nodded, absorbed in his chopping and mixing.

"Why are you leaving? Going up to Oregon, you said?"

"Oh, well, I was before in Mexico, and before that in Guatemala."

"Did you work there?"

"Yes, a little, but the Mexicans work for very little, so I came here," he laughed, "for the American green." He rubbed two fingers together with the grin still grinning and the blue eyes now widening out of the dark, bearded cheeks below the black halo of his hair. "Green American money." And we both laughed.

"I know what you mean." I still had my punk-rock slogans on my tee-shirt, but lately I'd been unfaithful I knew. It was gray, slow, and airy in that back room: a long Sven Nykvist tracking shot from an early Bergman film, or a typically symmetrical Antonioni long shot depicting the alienated decadent face to face with the humble country peasant, the busy worker standing, and the idle artiste sitting across the table watching him work. If I'd thought about it, I guess I would have felt a little bit embarrassed. Still, we lived in the same shit neighborhoods in the same town and worked the same shit jobs in order to survive.

Enrique came in then, his hair still wet, perfumed, and all dressed up to go out. "So, did you show him the room and everything?"

"Uh-huh," the Italian and I nodded together, frankly.

"Yeah," I began, trying to be polite. "I think the room is just too small for all my stuff." Only the night before I'd been up in Pacific Heights charming two guys with the same politeness, and I'd have that place for the same rent as this one (!), unless the third guy, who I hadn't met, decided for sure that he'd rather have a woman move in. But Pacific Heights, although lovely, was a little like going back to the suburbs.

Enrique smiled at me and said, "I thought so. Didn't you read, on the sheet, it said that the room was small?" He kept smiling but spoke toward the wall, as if I'd already gone but was still able to hear his insinuation that I probably thought I was too good for their apartment. I didn't remember their listing saying anything about the size of the room, but I'd looked at like a thousand listings that day.

"Yeah, I did," I stood up, "but I've lived in places where I could keep some of my stuff in the living room or something, and I thought it was worth a look." I was only just beginning to realize how easy it'd been to talk to and charm the guys in Pacific Heights the night before and how boring and stupid it would be living up there with them. But here I was kinda lost.

Enrique smiled even broader when I tried to shake his hand, but that was fine 'cause I really didn't want to shake his hand, only I didn't know what else to do. "I didn't want to just run off, you know, so I waited 'til you got out of the shower to tell you in person." As we spoke, the Italian sang along with the record that was still blasting in the living room, adopting a kind of southern accent in imitation of the boring rock band's boring singer. I only became conscious then that we'd been shouting the whole time.

Finally I got to the door, Enrique still smiling, insulting me without insulting me, not saying anything anymore. The Italian winked at me as I fled. I threw a smile in his direction, went down the hall, out, and back up the street to the corner. It hadn't warmed up much yet, but you could feel the sun coming. I could even see a little patch of sky out over the bay where the fog had already been blown away, so I walked off toward it, up Folsom Street, in the direction of the bay and the South of Market piers. I didn't have any more appointments that day, and I wanted to think about all of the places that I'd looked at so far. There was one place in North Beach where I'd been interviewed that I wanted really badly, and there was always the place up in Pacific Heights, I guess.

As I crossed over the crest of Rincon Hill, the fog started breaking up right over my head, moving fast in the breeze, and the sun came out at last. I stopped, took off my overcoat, and tilted my face up toward the underbelly of the Bay Bridge, which was huge and plastic-looking and right on top of me now, casting its shadow the other way, over toward the financial district, to feel the heat of the sun. I looked down at the piers and saw that two of them, just to the right of the bridge, had been leveled by fire.

I'd seen it on the news a few weeks before, but hadn't been down here since then and had forgotten that there had been a fire. Two long docks of black debris poked out into the greenish water, part of a steel infrastructure still leaning—black lines like a silhouette—on the cement foundations. Next to the site of the disaster, off to the edge of Third Street, a tacky-looking little bar and grill called The Boondocks sat with what must be a great view of the disaster out of its back windows, I thought. So I walked down there, went in, asked for a beer, and sat down in a booth in the back by the windows to look out at the devastated piers and the almost fluorescent green water warming in the sun. The waves here were just the tiniest little lines coming in absolutely evenly and then breaking apart against the pylons down under the bar somewhere.

"Beautiful day, isn't it?" the waitress asked, coming close enough for me to see that she was older than I had thought—watching her come in earlier, talking and joking with the regulars up at the bar—but she did a good job of hiding it by smiling and chatting happily all the time and using a lot of makeup.

"Yeah, it was cold when I was out there, and then it got sunny as soon as I came in here." We were both looking out the windows at the burnt-out piers. "That's something."

"Sure is," she said. "Did you see that little place right on the edge of it?" About ten feet from the black pavement and charred piles of debris sat a sad-looking little diner called Red's Java House.

"Yeah, he must have been sweating; well, I guess you people probably were too."

"Oh, I didn't work here then. But they said that it got hot." She reached out, touching her palm flat against the glass of the window in front of me. "That if you touched the window, it could burn you."

5/1984
San Francisco

Don't you dare quench my insatiable boredom
in yr breathtaking clothes, that mask you wear
on the back of yr head — bang
that tambourine, Dick! Evolution
makes you taller. Tempting terrain
of pissed-on boots, aquiline noses
and the return of knickers
,boxers, and big-bra biddies
moving off toward the powder
keg in the backroom where the tap is
                              always dripping.

Mustache man falters with the cigarette
bit, bumble nose boy weaves
,not looking, past his mascara
lips lubing the slick beer stem,
spittle warming the cool glassy knob.
Face powder becomes your holy-
cost, hologram, hot-toddy thump
of the mechanical bass on the lower breast
                    bone.

                    Touch
          and go, porno sonorous gaydar
has released all of our mysteries to the wheel
but for the odor. Rawer meat
and standing water. Heat comes down
a fool to her weight, pats herself off
to it. Aglow, I spy Ms. Dreamy beneath the telephone

light, before the piss-pots. Having
been groomed by the doorman, shy abdicates
my face to the wall: flower pot
caught in the hoar-frost. Hep hep me
realign 'er, get her offa that harp, 'at ship
of our ingenuity sailing to some higher service
out of a blinding night as white as this
to that great, golden
fuck up in the sky.

6/16/1992
San Francisco
(Kennel Club, née VIS, now Independent)

A SOUND FOR INFIDELITY

When she drops it down in front of him, the clack of the plate on the linoleum counter puts it into the picture: a scoop of paper-white ice cream globbed onto the plate as if fallen from a great height. Like the sound of "à la mode." Landing on the unfortunate pie wedge with a thud. A plop? It reminds him of the wet towels sliding off of the line and squooshing onto the cement floor of the basement in the dark below the house where he grew up. Pleasant Hill, California. He shouldn't have been playing down there, but the smooth basement cement against his bare feet was like around the swimming pool — only it smelled damp, of rotting laundry detergent instead of hot chlorine water evaporating in the sun and the dry heat, your hands sucked empty by sun and towels.

Looking now at the sprawled slice of apple pie crushed beneath the lump of imitation ice cream.

"You don't want that heated, do you?" the waitress had asked skeptically.

"Yes; please," he'd said.

— A fine start. Now —

"More coffee?"

"Please."

His lukewarm fork splits the slippery orb into two half domes; one's left standing while the other's melting bottom drags it off to the side of the pie and onto the dishwasher-hot plate. He remembers camping on the floor of Yosemite Valley with Mary last summer: his girlfriend? His fiancée? It was cold and warm at the same time, without flavor.

Anyway, he'd broken the vase Mary had given to him as a housewarming present for his downtown studio the day before — its black ceramic surface splitting a flat side against the beige carpet when he'd tipped it off of the table. Having to watch it fall was painful, his hands unable to arrest the momentum gaining as it rushed toward gravity's embrace. "Spak," it said, but with a thud, too, on the ratty old wall-to-wall carpet. Probably his groan had made it sound like a stomach being punched, like anything other than what it was: like teenagers fooling around in the parking lot when the scary guy gets bored with just teasing and pushes somebody into the juniper bushes, or the sound of the victim's butt coming down on the turf islands between the sidewalk and the black-top parking spaces. No, cooler than that — a late afternoon in the fall, long shadows, walking home alone after baseball practice. He'd been late to work — no time to pick up the pieces. (They're gone when he gets home.)

A mouthful of hot gluey pie filling and cold flavorless ice cream liquefying in his mouth brings him back to the diner. Lunch hour: the murmur of Muzak and voices slithering in and out of booths.

Chewing now, he remembers those things that Bridget had made him eat before going to work that time, turning them over in the pan, a fiasco that'd made them laugh together. He hadn't been able to understand what they were called through her accent:

"What are those things again?"

"---"

"What?"

"---"

"What?"

"Submarines! Did I say it wrong?"

Slices of white bread slipping around in the butter slick with holes cut out of their mealy centers. Giggling, Bridget drops eggs into the holes where they fry. She lifts them high in the air while he gets up from the kitchen table and lobs lumps of butter under the airborne submarines. She slams them back into the pan on their heads (caught fish flopping onto the deck of a ship at the end of jerking lines) while he stands close by thinking, now! Arms around her night-gowned middle; lips on the back of her neck. But the spatula and butter in his hands simulate chivalry and encourage chastity. Their uncomfortable silence then — filled with slow sizzling.

They're in the living room — breakfast seeming to hover upon the glass table — when he remembers having dreamed the meal some months before. "I was sitting here with a woman I didn't know, because I didn't know you then. I just now thought, 'I have to go to the bathroom,' and, as soon as I thought that, I went through it in my mind, getting up, walking down the hall, going through the door and into the bathroom. And I knew I'd done it before, in a dream, it must have been a year or so ago."

"Is it 'dreamed' or 'dreamt?'"

They talk about that, then —

"I still haven't cleaned the other bathroom yet so you'll have to go straight through the hall in my bedroom to my bathroom."

"I know."

Getting up now — interchangeable with the dream, he thinks, in the coffee shop, remembering over the now melding pie and ice cream slick — and building momentum toward the bedroom. Later, he knows now, it'll be with her. At first only to give the less-than-innocent (on both their parts) backrub after their long day's night: the after-lunch nap. Although she seems at times almost too innocent to be suggesting the seduction that she has to be suggesting. Well, flirting with herself maybe. They sweat out the nearness of it for a couple of weeks. He finds her disgusting perfume on his hands, and it gives him a hard-on at work. "Skin lotion," she tells him. "Not perfume."

Down the hall then and into her bedroom together for the first time. She's recently torn up the carpet for the hardwood beneath; this is where the sound of his step changes. This floor should have been the vase-shattering surface, he thinks, or the cold tile of the bathroom itself where he sits to pee, smelling and inspecting her lotions, brushes, and bric-a-brac.

Another lunch hour, he lies across the foot of her bed, smoking, while she takes a nap, her feet flat against his ribs. Staring at the backs of the blinds, he taps away ashes, remembering his parents skinny-dipping at night when they thought he was asleep. In the dark living room he'd felt only comfort and the thrill of being un-policed about his sleeping hours. Now, knowing Freud, he tries desperately to make his parents' nudity into some kind of trauma.

Walking back to work, he muses upon how ugly most people are when eating or sleeping. He tries to go through the dream again, but it's been replaced by the fact. Now he knows who the woman is and why he'd dreamt about her hallway. Fear? The rooms are a maze (that is, a passageway with a formula) leading to something — not the bathroom. Why does it feel cowardly not to want to go all the way through it to the end?

While he's gone pissing, she picks up the dishes, and he comes back to find her in the kitchen. Watching her wash, work, he thinks of the politics of their relationship. She's an Irish national, would like to have a green card, is exploited at her nursing job, an orphan besides. She grew up in a Gaelic-speaking nunnery and is only now, in San Francisco, learning English.

With complicity, then, in the diner, he digs into the pie crust with his fork, stirs the whole disaster into one sticky substance. The smarmy *click-clacking* of his fork against the plate. If I didn't know her here or if she'd known me there. But she's never been free before. "The orphanage," he mutters, sarcastically.

She raises her head up after her nap, and they talk, her feet still against his side. Intimacy is too easy behind the blinds: If only he had somewhere else to go besides work! They roll together with words, slowly as he walks to the back of the apartment again in his mind, one room at a time, trying to remember what he found there in his dream. Nothing. He goes back to work, the smell of her lotion rubbed into his clothes.

The events have no time scheme in front of his pie-wedge ice cream ball soup. Lunch finished, dessert under the big clock in Hentgen's Coffee Shop counts down the minutes: nearly time again for work. Like the clock beside her bed that ticks away their kissing. She's just going to take a nap, that's all. He can follow if he wants. He lies across the foot of the bed with cigarettes, making out the white outline of the sun between the blinds.

Raising the expected cup, adding more coffee, he looks at the waitress thinking, "Sexual politics." Says, "Thank you," to the raised arm weighted with a dangling, wrist-latched coffeepot. He pulls his cup back from the lip of the counter to its rightful spot above and to the right of the plate, "and cooking," he thinks.

But when had he dreamt that dream? A year ago maybe? Had he been seeing Mary yet then? Must have been, since it was almost two years ago now since they'd first met at the fund-raiser. That was back when Mary had been a volunteer at the organization. There he was, predicting the future again. His very own Cassandra. What would this sound like, he wonders, imagining: slamming the full coffee cup down onto the counter. Hardly break it, just splashing liquid and the ceramic clack dull against the soft Formica—hot coffee gurgling onto his clothes.

It's the frustration of seeing it happen the next time that he and Bridget'll be alone together. She'll let him come into her room, her bed, and then her body— it's like that for her; she actually believes that she'll only be letting him in. And it's infuriating because she's so well orchestrated her desire. It'll be the first time with another since he'd been seeing Mary. And they'd been talking about getting serious too.

Dropping the coins for the tip, flat-handedly slapping them onto the Formica lunch counter: a pickax taking out a chunk, chipping out a ragged splinter of cement from a solid block

4/4/1987
San Francisco

PARIS, 1986

We could all be
       —beautiful—
if it weren't for our situations

We must be
       —accidentally—
Slaves.

      1986
      Paris

PIAZZA INDIPENDENZA

She's drawing in her Pink Panther elementary-school copybook. They sell them in big piles on tables at the Oviesse, along with the neon-colored Evicta backpacks. That's where she probably got the bleach too. But that was weeks ago, and the roots are well grown out. She fingers the tips of the tangled strands about her collarbone with her left hand while her right hand, drawing a palm tree, plows right through the paper.

She stops.

Her mouth twitches. She wonders if it twitches all of the time or only when she notices it twitching.

She flips to a further page and begins to draw a heart, remembering how cold it had been last night in the park in the fog. But there really isn't much of a point in going any further south. Rome is more difficult, and the weather's probably about the same as here. It's been winter in Paris for more than a month. Ha!

Her cappuccino cup has been dry for a while now. She had gotten it up at the counter, paid first, and then taken the coffee over to a table and sat down — as if there wasn't an extra fee for table service — but nobody had said anything to her about it.

The old hunchbacked guy comes in and goes around the counter and into the back room. It's more casual around here, off the tourist track, this side of the central market and in back of the train station. Via Faenza, etc.

She bustles around now, gathering up her papers and notebook and putting on her big yellow raincoat. No one pays any attention to her when she goes back into the other room.

The hunchback comes back around the bar and orders a coffee. He nods to everyone, drinks it off, pays, and leaves.

She comes back, after a while, and gathers up her belongings again, during a lull in business, when almost all of the tables in the café are empty. She goes and stands in the doorway for a long time.

It's just getting dark.

Her mouth is twitching again. She gets lost somewhere in the bright violet BAR PATRIARCA sign across the street.

She turns abruptly, then, to the pleasant couple standing at the counter, smiles and says, "Bon soir!"

"Buona sera," the woman behind the cash register replies politely, cheerfully even, but without looking up.

The French junkie steps down off of the curb and wanders cat-a-cornered across the intersection.

10/27/1989
Florence

SUDDEN-DEATH

He sees "THE SEX DANCE" spray-painted in red by some American hand on the black back door of the most frequented discotheque in town. He's walking around Amsterdam again, having to look, being looked at, still waiting to get out, hide inside some safe hostelry. He's walking around the arc of each canal, or outward, down the straight streets that go between the station and the faraway suburbs. He goes to the park, sits in the autumn sunlight, gets up, and walks back to the station. The canals are concentric circles forming rings around the old city center — never touching it, or each other — that empty out into the swamp behind the city's back: the Single, the Man's Canal, the Prince's Canal, the King's Canal. The straight streets fan out like goosefeet on his map, the spaces between them widening as they drive inland.

He imagines it's his American stubbornness sustains him, despite the Anglophilia inherent in his Doc Martens etc., even as he's passing the place where he spoke to the pimp, the bench where he slept when he first ran out of money, the shop where he bought the loaf of bread and cheese that he had to make last until his money arrived. And he's still waiting. It's like the city's a roulette wheel; you lose at first but keep on raising the stakes to get it back, playing on, always a little behind and trying to catch up, like it's a sudden-death game.

Before, he'd met a young French woman who was eating off of the Hare Krishnas. He meets her in the morning, after the first night he's spent on the bench; he runs into her again in the park, the day he finally convinces the bank teller that he's going to die from exposure if she doesn't cash his "international" travelers check, but before that.

"Maybe I can help you because I've got a house." Either the Krishnas have set her up with a house, set up a house for her to live in with water but no electricity, or she's founded a squat on her own. She gives him the address. He remembers the ball of her pen rolling around the line of the street on his complimentary tourist map. There are marks all over it now, creases cracking through the printed circles of canals, straight lines of streets. "Come tonight if you still need a place."

They share his bread and cheese for lunch. "That was good. I didn't have any breakfast. I feel really bad when I don't get my breakfast." She also gives him the Krishnas' free food address for dinner. "But maybe you won't like it because they put drugs in the food."

"What kind of drugs?"

"Oh, maybe not so much. Anyway, maybe I like it."

Having read Poe when younger, Ballard, and Orwell, having bought all the Joy Division twelve-inch singles for every non-LP B-side, having owned an exclusively red-and-black wardrobe, he glares at the red lights above the women in their windows, or the closed red curtains that signify occupancy, brightly dressed tourists browsing, cars backed up on the narrow cobblestone streets, bicycles negotiating the interstices. Pedestrians knock knees against bumpers and fenders, cameras clicking, smelling the piss rising up from the doorways—he begins to see the city as Prospero's castellated abbey in "The Masque of the Red Death."

He'd thought: romance! A broke American in a foreign city (Henry Miller, the lure of—). Now the all-too-predictable turns of this narrative rise up like specters before him, one after the other, like Prospero's colored rooms or a twisted railroad flat back in New York City. Only he's not in control here. He's uncomfortable (cold). He's bored (walking). It's degrading (boring). He'd been attracted to the game, but doesn't know how to play from behind; games are only formulas of degradation for the losers. He'd always done the usual thing; saying, "Sure," to a boss, "Okay," to his parents, "All right, I will," to his friends. This was only around again another thing that fewer people ever get to, but not few enough to make it special. A ring around the rosy. He turns another corner, wondering: when do we all fall down?

"This is our doorway," the sign says, "please don't piss in it."

He's staked out a bench, away from the red lights, to sleep on; it's a larger, flatter bench than the regular city issue, in front of a pub. Inside, the jukebox is playing The Platters' "Great Pretender."

The police make them all leave the train station at one in the morning. He'd felt like prey there anyway. Watching carefully the crazy skinhead who lifts his feet absurdly high when walking back and forth between the station's garbage cans, eyeballing him threateningly on each useless circumlocution. Like a bobbing horse on a merry-go-round, he thinks, smiling, affronting the serious skinhead who meets his eyes then.

Then the Irish junkie who's only there to keep his silent friend company — the friend's waiting for his girlfriend to come back — starts lecturing. The girlfriend's gone off "with some old dildo" for enough gilders to get their heroin for the night so they'll be able to sleep.

"We've got a caravan, I mean, you could come back and sleep with us, but I don't think you'd like it very much, you know, with a bunch of junkies." He'd said before: "I'm not kidding, look! I'm not kidding you, I've got to get it, look!" Rolling up his sleeve to expose two tiny white dots on red and puffy blotches. Show and tell; costume of the red death? "Look at my eyes. I've aged five years in the last year." When the junkie tugs on his eyelid for emphasis, exposing the red flesh that usually slides, hidden, against the eyeball, is when he first imagines that the fatal guest has arrived, that Prospero's party might be coming to its inevitable end.

He gives the desperate Irishman a sip out of his water bottle because — "I don't want to have to drink out of the john, you know ..." — he knows that it costs money just to get into the john. "Hey, I'm clean!" He rubs a squeaking finger across his front teeth.

He pulls two leftover cigarettes from Copenhagen out for the junkie and his friend, and it's, "My wife's Danish; if she saw me now, she'd never recognize me."

A street act always comes around: juggling, playing on tattered guitars, fire eating—all of Prospero's deliciously Arabesque entertainments. "You know, most people, if you tell 'em you want it for smack, they won't give it to ya." The forlorn pause, then pity for his friend—who's since paced off across the platform—for having to watch his girlfriend go off with the "old dildo." Then, when the junkie's through with the particulars of the situation, he digresses into a general, undirected disgust for the "whole fucking weird scene" there at the station and then back home at the "caravan."

"It's hell in there, itching all night, a bunch of junkies all rolled together; a fucking caravan in Amsterdam. You know," he pantomimes, scratching like a monkey, "we've got fleas."

He gets away from the Irish junkie by having to put another gilder in the locker holding his luggage, which is necessary once every twelve hours, to keep it from springing open. Nine guilders left this first night he spends on the street. The policewoman asks him, "Are you waiting for a train tonight?"

"---"

There aren't any more trains out of Amsterdam after one.

"Then you'll have to leave." Leaving, he passes behind the skinhead who's looking suspiciously at the departure schedule. Glancing over his shoulder, he goes back to his bench. Inside the pub the jukebox is playing "Heartbreak Hotel."

Too much time to think while walking the lines (streets) back and forth between the station and nowhere, around and around the canals 'til we all fall down tired on a bench again in the park (during the day while it's still open). Where are the ashes, ashes? He watches the scenic canal water, walks with the flow or against, stinking brown and green below the bridges. There's decay where junkies claim to be clean and look healthy. Round and round we go, but where she stops, nobody knows. (All the happy faces pouring out of the station at each train's arrival.) "But," the French woman laments, "old faces just seem to disappear. I don't know if they leave Amsterdam, or what." "She just," the pimp will tell him, his hand going out, making a spiral downward, "you know, like this."

She, the French squatter living off of the Hare Krishnas' free food, takes him to the public library where you can sit and read the periodicals for nothing. "When I came home last night — you know, I'm letting these German people stay at my house. They are musicians. They were all sitting around in the dark, talking, or doing whatever they were doing. But I saw that it was metaphoric for the situation, you know? I know that it is money that will turn the lights on, so to speak." They walk and she speaks philosophy softly and deliberately in her second-hand English, and he isn't sure if he doesn't understand her words because she's talking nonsense or if he isn't hearing everything she says.

"You see, I project onto them and then they project something back onto me, which makes me project something back onto them, and that's just an endless set of mirrors."

They pass a houseboat where she claims to have known the people who'd rented it, but they've disappeared. "In jail probably."

"Stuck," he finds himself thinking (if he could afford to send a letter he'd write one), "in Amsterdam."

He goes out the lines alone, having left the French woman at Bob's Youth Hostel where she's found some horny American boys willing to share their pot with her. Then the circles carry him back around to the Damrak, the station, and the main square with the silty, reed-filled lagoon at its back. Marking off, little by little, each day in his travel datebook; he catches a railroad cop looking over his shoulder at the row of X's. Anyway, he was still alive during each and every day that he lives long enough to cross out.

Another gilder for his luggage, another twelve hours under lock and key, then back to the bank along one of the canals. It turns out to be the wrong bank communicated to him from home; his money's still in Copenhagen. "I'm still stuck," (closed over the weekend) "I guess, for a couple more days at least."

He goes away after they finally cash his check—now that they know he's got other money on the way to cover it—to stop his crying breakdown in front of the other customers. He takes his cash and goes to the park again; anyway, he'd seen all the museums before his money ran out.

Must have, somehow, wanted it, willed it inside. Could have called the States earlier. Could have been more irate at the bank, got them checking the other banks in Copenhagen sooner. "Okay, if there's nothing, I'll just come back tomorrow," he'd said over and over.

He'd let it slide away in his American stoicism, walled himself up inside of a fantasy castle against the danger outside and then invited it in, leaving himself exposed and out on the streets.

He wakes up at dawn, wet and shivering on the bench by the canal in the fog. He realizes: I'm awake(!) and sits up like a shot. His bag's still there, had been under his head all night. And he's alive!

Writing letters he can't afford to send, finally, just to have some company. Maybe they'll be found later, he jokes to himself. Shivering, muscles clenched that he can't get to let go, he walks around the loop again, along the canal to the youth hostel. He waits outside for three hours, smoking the last of his Danish cigarettes, and then sneaks inside while the front desk is mobbed with people checking out. Anyway he'd been staying there before his money had run out and looks more or less the same as all the other backpackers and students — he won't be noticed at the ball. Inside, he shaves and showers long under the hot water. Walking out, he's as tidy as any other tourist, despite all of his hipster camouflage.

Then it's back to the straight streets, past the Single, the Man's Canal, the King's Canal, and the Prince's Canal. Back to the bank on the last day before his present money would run out, and he'd be on the streets. Thinking of it like a play-off, a sudden-death game. But it's not. He walks out of the bank and back onto the same streets in the same day in the same city. It's just that he doesn't have any money anymore, can't get back into the hostel to sleep. Other than that, nothing's changed.

When he gets back to his bench after having been forced out of the train station, there's someone sitting on top of the backrest, his feet on the seat, smoking a cigarette. This guy's bicycle is leaning up against the bench. Too tired to keep on walking and to look for another bench, he sits down anyway, and they look at each other but don't speak.

Later, when the pimp pulls out another cigarette, he has to ask for a light. The ice broken, he also asks, "Are you waiting for someone?"

"No."

The pimp takes his matches and lights up, waits a moment, looking off down the street across a bridge over the canal, then hands the matches back.

"Are *you* waiting for someone?"

"Yes. One of my ladies. She is working. Where are you from?"

"New York." He's referring to the state, but is thankful for the ambiguity.

"A wonderful city. I visit there for three days once." The pimp's English is curt, simplified.

"Where are you from?" He's a skinny dark man with long hair and a beard.

"Peru. I have political asylum from the days of Alvarado."

The pimp speaks, still looking down the street that humps up over the canal and goes off, a dotted line of streetlights, toward the periphery. "I hope she makes enough so that we don't have to do any others tonight. You see, I have three ladies working for me; they are all hooked on this heroin. I, myself, have managed to get down to one injection of cocaine per day." He doesn't say it proudly, either for the horror of it or the implied reformation in progress, but more like a bored actor playing an expository scene, like the darkened faces in documentaries or confessionals — just the facts, ma'am.

He has the nonchalant air they all put on when being most dramatic. A command performance? The various costumed guests arrive, one after the other, displaying their finery, until the death's head rises up out of the crowd and strolls past the prince himself. Were they all trying to tell him what they think he wants to hear?

It's even more boring at night; canals black below bridges, red lights in windows showing women showing their tongues or reaching inside their corsets to flop a breast out at you. They walk along the Damstraat dressed to the hilt on their way to the disco. Everyone's come to party; "Come high," the sign says outside the Hard Rock Café, "leave higher!" American soldiers pass, stoned, in groups. "Where I come from back home in the States, no mother-fucker messes with me," one hears, again and again, in passing.

"All the girls are hooked on this heroin. You know, just the other day, one," the pimp pantomimes putting a needle in his arm, "she, you know, like this." He rolls his head to the side, closes his eyes, and lets his tongue loll out. Then he lifts his head back up, takes a drag on his cigarette, shrugs and says, "Just like that. Dead."

"The big disco is called the Melkweg I hear. Have you been there yet?" Spray painted on the back door it says, "THE SEX DANCE." Later, when he's back at the youth hostel, someone dismisses his nights on the street with, "You could have gone into one of the discos, you know, to stay warm. They're open all night, and you don't have to buy anything. Anyway, it's fun."

"Do the girls in the street make as much as the ones in the windows?"

"Usually more. The price is the same, but the ones in the windows must pay for their checkups and things."

The jukebox in the pub behind them is playing "The Lion Sleeps Tonight."

"I see, no overhead."

The pimp smiles. "So, why then are you sitting on this bench tonight?"

"I was going to sleep here. I scoped this bench out for sleeping on earlier today when I was walking around; it's bigger and flatter than the regular city benches."

"Yes, it is an okay bench." The pimp doesn't have to look at it to say this; he's still looking down the street after his lady. "But don't you have a hotel?"

("They want you to be a good tourist, that is all," the French woman had told him. "You have to have money to pay for your freedom.")

"No, I don't. I've been waiting for some money to arrive, but there's been a problem with the banks, and I've run out of money while waiting."

"You have no credit card?"

Listening, he realizes that he's acting now, too, is embarrassed to be explaining his stupidity to someone who's survived more than he'll ever imagine. He's only toying with disasters that others actually live. How did he ever wangle this invitation to the masque? An unnamed minor character, he too-humbly dresses himself in the motley of the fool.

Again, during the endless days of waiting between the nights spent on benches, he walks the arc of each canal, starting at the center and circling further and further outward. Passing a couple, thinking of sex because they're kissing passionately, and the woman, her back to him, is lifting the edge of her blouse to scratch herself just above the waistband, exposing a slice of her very white flesh. He's wondering why it turns him on when he passes them, and, in passing, smells death on them. It's the smell of the hall in the apartment complex outside the door where he'd delivered newspapers when he was a boy, where one of his customers had died inside her apartment. It's probably just the smell of some kind of disinfectant—it doesn't smell natural, like decay, but more chemical, like a preservative—but it was death to him all the same.

Now all he smells is the pimp's cigarette smoke floating lazily around them as they sit in the damp night air above the omnipresent canal.

"I have a place. I have a room, you know, up above our flat that you could stay in tonight. Usually I rent it, but, you know, the last person I had up there was a speed freak, and he made too much noise all the time doing things, so now it is empty. Because, you know what you risk sleeping on this bench? The police may come along. They will ask you what you are doing. You will say, 'I am sleeping,' and they will take you to the police station. They may not keep you for very long when you explain to them that you're waiting for your money to arrive, but they worry about people who have no money. They think that people who have no money do crazy things."

"Look," he tells the guy at the desk of the Christian youth hostel, "I don't want to spend another night on the streets."

No one's looking him in the eyes here. The place is called "The Shelter."

"Can I give you some kind of collateral?"

"---"

"I'll be getting my money tomorrow, the day after at the latest."

"---"

"My passport, my driver's license?"

"What good are those to me?"

"You know I won't be leaving without them."

"Do you have anything of value?"

"My watch?"

"Okay, I'll give you one night's credit on the watch. Sheets are on the bed."

Then the clerk's filling out a card for him with the room and bed number. "And I want you to read this—" It says, "This is a Christian youth hostel. That means that we want to share the good news of Jesus Christ with you!" After that, it's just a list of rules. When he's read the rules through, he fills out the guest card, which must be filled out, by law, in every hotel or hostel in the Netherlands.

"And I'd like to give you this." (A pamphlet of quotations from the Book of Luke.)

"Thank you." He carries the blanket upstairs and goes to sleep for sixteen hours.

He crosses the four canals out to the big park. He sits there every day, waiting for his money to arrive, eating from his loaf of bread and slab of cheese, trying to read a novel by Samuel Beckett, but he can't seem to concentrate. He walks back through the rings, stopping at the bank on the Man's Canal to see if there's any word on where his money is. "I'm sorry, Mr. Alland, but, you know, sometimes things don't go just as we plan them."

"But they said it would only take two days."

"That's what they always say."

The pimp's Dutch girlfriend frowns when she comes up to the bench in front of the pub, and the smoking Peruvian and the silent American sitting there motionless. "You've been waiting here all this time? I've been over on the bridge, waiting for you! This creep was following me—"

"You didn't make any sign when you went by."

"Yes, I did. I went like this with my hand for you to follow."

"I didn't see it then. This is a friend, an American. I told him he could sleep in the room upstairs tonight."

She frowns, shaking his hand.

"He's all right," the pimp says. "Did you get enough?"

"Yes."

"We must go and pick up the heroin now."

"There's three of us now; that means we can't use the bicycle. It is not a good place to walk in."

"You've got to know very well the people on the street," the pimp had been telling him before, "or else you get the bad stuff and—" He'd pantomimed the dying whore again.

He'd been walking away from the Christian youth hostel, just coming up to the Nieumarkt, when a woman with clean bandages and a splint along her wrist had said something to him that he hadn't been able to understand.

"I'm sorry. I don't speak Dutch."

"Do you want to go with me?" She'd smiled at him sweetly then, not realistically at all, childishly. In the park, eating the hard-packed health-food bread, in rations to make it last, he has to admit to himself that he'd believed in that smile.

"No. Thank you anyway. I haven't got any money."

The French woman living off of the Hare Krishnas' free food is named Jennifer. Her parents are English, she tells him, but she'd been raised in a suburb of Paris. She's, technically speaking, a citizen of both countries. She tells him that, "My family are all cowards; that is the only word that I can use to describe them."

"Why?"

"They were so afraid of me. And when my mother died, they just wouldn't have anything more to do with me."

Jennifer is hoping for some money of hers to arrive from friends in Paris who've been "looking after some business of mine for me." Her papers had been stolen, pickpocketed out of her purse while she'd been eating in a restaurant a month or so before. She'd been arrested in Paris that last spring, she confesses, around the same time he'd been there, just after arriving in Europe, six months ago.

"Why are you living in Amsterdam?"

"Because here I can smoke. In England or France, they would put me in jail. Here they don't care. In America it is the same, no? You can smoke there."

"Pretty much."

"It is not legal, but it is permitted, no? They don't like it in France; they think that it destroys their precious unity."

She takes him to Bob's Youth Hostel where he leaves her with a group of American college boys who, allured by her French accent and superior attitude, are getting her stoned.

Back in the park, he passes a couple on a bench shooting up. The woman has her bone-white arm bent, her fist clenched tight, a needle stuck upward, not very deeply, into the underside of her forearm. A bright red trail of blood is coming out of the hole and making its way toward her elbow. Her boyfriend watches it up close, smiling and laughing, he supposes, at his girlfriend's rudimentary medical skills.

"You always have to pay for pussy," some loud American pontificates along the Damstraat, to his friends. "You pay for the clothes, the shoes, the hair products and cologne; you pay to get into the disco, you pay for her drinks, and you pay for the hotel room or the car to take her home."

"You have to pay for the rubbers too!"

"Damn straight."

The pimp and his girlfriend tell him to go down, to the left, all the way down to the second street on the left, across the bridge. They're going to pick up the heroin and meet him there at the end of that street. "We will pick you up there — it is a long way down, but go all the way to the end." They ride off in the Dutch fashion, the woman sitting sidesaddle on the bike-rack behind the seat.

He's walking down the long street then, alone in the dark. The bridges hump up, in turn, over each circle, over each canal. He's going away again from the center, the station, the city, and the waterfront at its back; he's more bored than he's ever been in his whole life. He studies the street itself as he walks, bag in hand, to the prearranged meeting place. He looks into the dark windows of bakeries, bookstores, galleries — places he might have entered and explored as a tourist with money. *Entre libre* the signs say in Paris. "You could go see the Anne Frank house, but most people go straight to the Red Light District." Nighttime changes everything. The city appears deserted; the long street is still, like a tableau built for his amusement alone, all of its treasures displayed behind a permanent pane of glass, like a picture frame—only enough light for his eyes to see the insides of the closed shops in black and white.

He does pass one or two other lone pedestrians; they walk looking down, glancing up at him as they pass. This is so stupid, he decides, because it isn't really anything. He'd been attracted to a nothingness that would now show no limit. Making mistakes had always been a joke before; you just shrugged and said, "So what?" or, "Sorry," made up for it however you could, and went on. It wasn't ever the end of the world. There'd been no climax, no resolve, or final curtain (from behind which the red death had stepped out and taken its bow), and that's why it was nothing, the same as anything else, stupid; it had no frame in which to become a story and present its moral. He finally comes to the end of the street and the couple come riding up to him right away, smiling.

"It is up around that corner there, the second street, above a café, number one. I will leave you the door unlocked."

"Just before you get there, you will see a blue light that says, 'Michelin'," adds the smiling prostitute sitting on the bike-rack as they ride off.

He finds the sign of the smiling, running, Michelin man. He finds the café, but the door to apartment number one is locked and there are four buzzers, four different flats in the building, and none of them are numbered. Maybe they forgot him, or maybe somebody else who lives in one of the other flats had come home between times and locked up. Anyway, it doesn't produce any reaction from him at all. He walks the long way back toward the center of town to his bench—only now he's worried about the police. He sees one of their cars go by on the other side of the canal so he moves to another, more concealed, regular city bench behind some parked cars overlooking the same canal. At first he jumps up to a sitting position every time a car lumbers by, and then there aren't hardly any more cars, and he only vaguely opens his eyes to watch their headlights graze him as they pass.

Later still, he hears a pair of shoes clicking along the street, then around behind the parked cars and right up to his bench. A guy with a bag of French fries in one hand and napkins in the other rests his elbows on the back of the bench and looks down at him. He's dressed really well, in a Las Vegas sort of way. "Hi!" he says.

"Hi."

A gold medallion is hanging off the man's chest and dangling in his face. Smiling, he offers his bag of fries: "Want some?"

"No thanks. I ate already."

"Where you from?"

"New York." Some consolation.

"Oh," the man says, settling his head down on top of his folded arms. There's a long silence then, all the way around the canal to the sea behind them, maybe even in the main square, the station itself darkened and closed by now, as if, for just these few moments before dawn, the whole city were finally asleep, all of its drugs taken, awaiting a new day. He thinks of the Melkweg and imagines the rhythm machine, like a heartbeat, flashing along with the strobe lights down below street level, keeping the otherwise motionless city alive. Later, the fellow raises his head up and opens his eyes, the medallion returning to its spot against his open shirt when he straightens up, pats him on the chest, and says, "Take care." He's asleep again before hearing the man's shoes carry him away along the canal.

He hears a car's motor then, and then another, a bicycle swishing by and someone sweeping. He cracks his eyes open and sees the sky beginning to turn purple out of the black. That means there's red in it, he thinks. The sun! And he's alive!

He runs into Jennifer at the post office after they've finally found his wire and feel comfortable cashing his money order. She says, "I'm quite cross." It seems that her money from Paris still hasn't arrived. "And now they tell me that since I don't have my papers, I couldn't pick up the letter anyway, even if it had come. Have you had breakfast yet?"

"Yes, at the hostel."

"I feel horrible until I have my breakfast."

He gives in: "I've got some bread and cheese again."

"I think I could do with that."

Before, when he'd had nothing, it had felt okay just sharing his last bread and cheese with her, but now that he's okay, he feels taken advantage of. That day she takes him to the library again, where you can read the English, American, and international papers for nothing and drink cheap coffee. It's on him.

10/15/1986
Bruxelles

LUBBOCK ELEGY (for Billy Boy)

Texas is a great hot
hollow balloon here
in Lubbock, a swollen
membrane; lethargic & frustrated
with bluegrass underfoot;
breezy and indifferent
storms pass, they soak
and they electrify
the red clay earth;
bobbing, here, at the end
of its tether, about
to feel that crack
of thunder; about to feel
one pair of feet fall
on its back, forever
and be gone, say, day
after day, after tomorrow;
and shudder in its own
slow rumble of thunder;
and be gone
forever

                    8/11/1993
                    Lubbock, Texas

SURVIVED BY

Heart strap
thread of renewal
blood through a mucus membrane
stop — it don't stop
thread through a needle's eye
wet throng of need
don't ever stop
need — the relative
      pronoun implying possession

        Demons
    in the boom box
    strung over shoulders
    resenting rhythms
    life's train
    can't derail
dare not stop
taking ways
away.

      9/14/1994
      NYC

ON TO THE ROTTEN ROAD TO TORONTO
(To See Patti Smith)

The forest kept coughing bloody woodchucks up onto the freeway's gray. Wayfarers doodled lewd remarks on sedimentary rock, their names and dates and dwellings, same as history's traces. Semis vied for steam, met rickety-winged bugs head on, bludgeoning glass shields slick across their faces. We phoned from a truck stop coddled by ivy, stopped to fuck at a roadblock, nothing like the book or movie. There were no safe stars on the killing deer's freeway, nature's night of long knives, radial tires, and FM radio.

We arrive and nobody's home there, no, here; cuffs and all hobble through this door to nostalgia. Toronto's got a hand on its crotch. Girls in love jockeying for position in front of the loaned stage, a chore to listen to the poseur. The other guest arrives finally and re-indicates our hateful loving chaos with a finger across a sealed crotch, a hush while the other hand traces a magic circle in sound, couched in the wastes of some hungry mouths what clean Ethiopia up. Chalk "Reno" on a sack of nada, stalactites of sand in its eyes, and the tits of style. (She slags off a country's stitches with gall and transcendence, pissing out her guts for the next world.)

This new freeway paved out before us leads out of air to the rapturous space we speak of in time without distance. Elude my bloating stomach—am I dead?—coming back divided from might's insistent posturing, larger in nighttime's sight lines. My roosting spirit stops—a lull—swoops up toward rapturous abandon above the lights and stinks of sweat. This new history traces building blocks for the turquoise tower of Babel kept hostage by the ruins of Berlin's wallowing. Languages mix, skimming the surface of our rebellious dystopian citadel struck down in time, our togetherness in the rebirth of the naive, having retreated again into basements and dreams, drugs and forgetfulness, impotence and peppermint.

This mixed-up us, constructed by the bodies working with the acoustic drum beat, enlists *kafirs* for a new caravan led by the poets of necrophilia whose Aztec boots kick a heartless corpse down the temple steps to the dogs of industry. Coming now for posterity, heads up toward these official suns, digging into the past for this particular resurrection, which is no longer allowed, the spoken songs of high rebellion shout out loud to the guitar's best razor-notes.

Same as history's traces, this moment, rewound, not shot in time, is mine. Now dominoes are tumbling in the spasmodic microcosm, planting seeds in two hundred Spartacus' dreams to be freed tonight—and tomorrow? Who knows?

6/1995
Toronto/NYC

PROSPECT PARK

I. THE BATTLE OF BROOKLYN

      Graves

first traces
    of America

    gouged
    into the hill here
        (ample hills
    of Whitman's Brokenland)
after fighting the battle
of Long Island, the battle of Brooklyn

    most likely
there were graves,
    cannonball hollows,
    foxholes, dug in
        colonists

    soldiers
carving sheathes into the earth
leaving liberty off
    for unsettling war
    to protect and obliterate
that foliate hill
    among hills

    Washington couldn't take it back
and America was driven away

from Brokenland Bay, from itself
    the first time
    by Bloodyback red

II. A DISTRICT

America came back, twice
    The renewed Union
triumphant to suburbanize
the Slope with an *arc de triomphe*
    and the row house

drawing grid-straight streets
for the newly united populace
    of north and south
    black and white
still sluggishly ferrying
    back and forth across
    the East River to New Amsterdam

    Manhattan to Brooklyn
    Brooklyn to Manhattan

reaching out and into
the river of cement overshoes

    the past in the future
    a future in the past

    wake in our faces,
    backing into the harbor

III. CROSSING BROOKLYN SUBWAY

The reality of these faces in the crowd

  black petals
  white petals
   on a wet gray bough

rush hour dozing
from train
  to platform
to stair

rising out the honeycomb and caverns
in the cement fabric
   (Odysseus
  pours blood into the troughs
   and the spirits
  come forward to speak)

beneath the Grand Army Plaza
  all our moving mingles
    until
the scattered faces segregate
tired to their exits and entrances
   (the gates of Hades
  are wide going in
   but narrow
  for those thinking to leave)

black faces turn north
white faces south

where the arch and avenue split
        the neighborhoods in two
a quiet architecture
of ill-repair

IV. CRASH LANDING

Henry McCaddin Seventh
        & Sterling
lifts the weight
bricks and formaldehyde
putty redoubles
        this rip in the fabric
of the neighborhood — these open
        wounds close up
        for business

V. BUMS

                dodging streetcars
the last traces of America
        left
with Ebbett's Field
where the slaughter-house pigs stank
        pink and blue
before a ballpark dressed them
Jackie, we asked too much
breaking the color barrier

his hair turned gray
              bums
              on a perfect
                     green blanket

VI. THE SLOPE

Not New Amsterdam
rather Van Dyke Slope, where
vagina to vagina, sheath to sheath
the New York family
reborn, constructs itself
beleaguered in the park
by the Flatbush division
a Mason-Dixon
of unsettled America, refugees
where we've lost
the first battle
the World Series
year after year
of the American Revolution
dodging streetcars
in Brokenland blue
'gainst Yankee stripes and Bloodyback red
dug in
a neighborhood
         for housing's next millennium

                    1993
                    Brooklyn, NY

'AT OLDE TRAIN IN VAIN
(House Hunting II)

The Ninety-Seventh Street gate, portals to the scraping underbelly of the beast. A hind leg. We're just fleas, sittin' up at the counter, sittin' up at the bar, getting' ready to eat. Gateway to out of control: Grand Central at its heart, the zoo you can't look at but only see to. "Yo, whas up? Whas up?" She can't hardly perch on them heels down skeleton row on her way to 110th Street, I guess, crackling commuter trestles, tombs, an end to torment. (That other junkie crying: her black-eyed boyfriend ex-Hell's Angel puts a silver bullet in her handbag 'n' stomps away in slow motion. Not getting' whatever it was 'at she was pleading to get she calls the hulk back with, "Hey! Fuckface!")

I'm beginning to feel awkwardly alone all these transitory days long. The waiter hates me writing up at his counter, pushes coffee, confused pancakes in my direction. Back o' the border, falling off a' the fork before reaching my mouth. Nodding on the platform.

"Do you know what time it is?" Stares. "Do *you*?" Salsa, soul, salsa, soul. No second cup a' coffee offered.

Anyway, she was teetering up by the playground through the George Washington houses. He let her go like a stage mother shoves her little girl out in front of a blind audience, listening, so you could hear her breathing; pushing her into that spotlight, the sun, in 95 degrees and 100 percent humidity, as if shorts were really the answer to those legs with barely enough fat on 'em to keep the bruises blue. *De rigueur* to ask for clean silverware here. Obligatory map of Greece. No second cup a' coffee unless yas ask.

Those fucking yuppies back at the Eighty-Sixth Street station spittin' at the rats down on the tracks while waitin' for the express train. They emerge from the movie set (very fifties, built for Doris and Rock and just left behind) that is Park Avenue and think that all their slumming is mostly doable downtown.

In comes a white "HOLLYWOOD" visor. You don't even know where she's goin'. "Yo." There comes another. "Whas up? Whas up?" A rolled-up newspaper cradle. Then a scuffed-up bike accident loser slumps onto a stool, too, and fumbles with the want ads.

Her boyfriend? "Gone," she says — pregnant pause — "long gone."

Walkin' in circles. It all stops if there's a cop stationed at the corner. "You can't touch *that*." Sleeping so huddled up for it, can only go with a nod, like last Christmas, and the icicles pointing down from under the trestles through the portals of what used to be Park Ave., like the subway's frozen teeth — commuter train — they all correct me. Ye olde el. Seriously too cold to get mugged, I thought.

Whatever it is that's your mission you go on into it; you don't just lie down and die, do ya? You put on your makeup and sway off across the borough, 'at bird 'at kept on fallin' off a' his wire and gettin' back up on to it. You listen to so many stupid conversations about the same damn bullshit, you get a little too eager to speak your mind. You left off the bra, got out the tank top, climbed up on them shoes and did what you had to do.

She might even climb up that steep slope just for the pleasure of being stared at, to say 'at she had done it once outside of the subway — anyhow it always ends in a fight, gettin' yourself thrown out, like you like it like that — oh, I like it like that. While I go racin' up outta that tunnel and into the blue September-light smear of the hazy day over Spanish Harlem. I go up like a shot light bulb, browned out in a power surge to a blazing new home. I call, but ain't got no.

Out the window and across the platform I saw the Virgin Mary, dripping blood of original sin, get on the wrong train. But I was so happy for her: now she's a woman.

I jes be feelin' so alone, doin' all these things I done so many other times before in so many other places.

I never even saw 111th street; is that fair?

9/30/1992
NYC

NYC AC or,
THE EFFECTS OF OSMOSIS ON ANOTHER
JOURNALIST'S PHILIPPIC ORGASM

(for M. T. and E. M.)

Vertical squeeze and the refuse blows, gets blown black again. Silenced humming appliances remind Saturday of some lost solitude. Instead, we go out, again—talking and reading, reading and talking. They write more words about fucking than fucking words. Plus the deranged barbarism of even your best friend to protect the pack when you refuse to buckle under.

Let revered teenage-years and words about fucking delude them into thinking that sex and drugs and rock 'n' roll are cooler than copyright: outside of style, a waste of time's only a waste of time. There's no arguing with content when the *tabula razza* is being raised like a fucking flag, forked in the ass, flipped over the flame, and gagged again; any waste of time's still only a waste of time. More words about fucking instead of doing it.

You buy Charles Atlas a drink; pilfering masculinity, he sits at your table, and HE WON'T EVER GO AWAY!

— you'll never be able to lift him.

But, hey, this is America, where even pretend (fill in the blank)s buy it because it smells like *Vogue* or it molds like plastic. They hang it on their multicultural holiday tree, trash it out onto the sidewalk when they're done, and set it on fire after New Year's Day. And it's always fucking New Year's Day in New York fucking City, always a party on Saturday night, when McSorley's meets the Life Café, and the people who pretend to see honesty in politics laugh common sense out of you with cocktail conversation and baseball bats in the Battery. They take out our uncertainty, our hes-hesitation, lay it on the table and eat, relishing the exalted moment of howling with the hyenas over the sensitive and subtle kill.

What do you know? *Wolfen* had it right.

Then they go home alone and write articles (about fucking) while you jerk off in the bathroom.

The freedom of elevators and AC is enough for this NYC fourth estate CIA shadow FBI. Sly sly sly. I read it on the way to work. I'm on my way, Good-bye.

8/22/1996
NYC

MORPHEUS

Red haze purple blessing alarms don't sound today
i can't get up the sun's so hot
on sister morphine's eyelids
along her way to all the heart-stopping o.d.s
in "tiny Greenwich village apartments"
living the New Science where
not speaking does something
to sleep's tyranny
while history's blue recycling bins
get dug through by philosophers of the needle,
philosophers of Tompkins Square Park
where the Shadow's pigs go mad
again in their circular, again in their weekly
and if you sleep too long you'll never get up
if you sleep too long you'll never get up
and every movie you see's just another *sonnifero* now
every button on the TV's another bitter
sleeping pill to swallow and the rich
are only happy 'cause the poor despise them
they don't own anything other than that
that's useful.

9/20/1994
NYC

CAZZO / BUCO (Rubato all'Antonin Artaud)

Venni al Central Park sotto l'ennesimo obelisco
cercando l'imperatore Eliogabalo
e la sua dea solare, la siriana
trasportata nel grembo dell'occidente
in piena luce della sua sacra sessualità, il cazzo solare
intagliato con uno dei visi di Shiva.
Governava Roma col potere di inghiottire
ogni potenzialità nel buio assoluto
del suo culo, il vorace orifizio di un Dio
assoluto e buco. Fu solo, solare, e folle.
Aveva quattordici anni.

       Ti cerco tutt'ora, senza la possibilità
di dormire, deluso con Morfeo
e tradito dal Priapo. Libero,
allora, dalle influenze del filosofo alato.
Cerco anch'io il buco più profondo
dietro il sole. I tuoi occhi.
U tambure suonò, e o munn`
s'alz' cumm' nu cazz'
eccitato dalla danza che poi
c'insegnava la delusione. Dentro l'alone
di fuoco — le fiamme inghiottiranno
tutto, sarà come la vita si vive e, vivendo,
si spegne. La volontà si iscrive qui.

Sdraiato sotto 'na pioggia di semi verdi volanti,
qui, al Central Park, o aspettando
all'uscio della buca nera che era il tuo tempio,
ti ricordasti

      Egitto;
Nut dipinta sopra il cadavere,
il sole fra le sue mani alzate
che, sporgendosi all'alba, dalla vagina sua
fatta da due mani, faccia a faccia
  ,dalla principessa tua madre,
   ti fece imperatore e ti uccise
coi suoi piani oscuri

   (ci sono sempre piani a Roma per Roma)
e siam persi in tale atti religiosi
,atti di fede, fatti martiri alla vita stessa.

      Poi quei visi scuri
dipinti sul legno per distinguere le mummie
ch'erano cittadini Romani...

Ti sdraiasti fra loro come l'impero
stesso, inaugurando nuovi costumi
di' fegato / di' cazzo.

     Raccogliendo i semi
dagli alberi della vita. Al tramonto
pregavi salvezza

dalla notte
femminile e le mani alzate—il sole vaginale
della dea della morte—che t'amavano.
Che lucente paura!

Notti senza sogni.

5/11/1994
NYC

STANCHEZZA

Allora le nuove didascalie si alzano qui, in questo spazio bianco sotto l'aquila romana che sta spezzando il suo cuore contro il muro della sua incapacità di ragionare in un universo né giusto né pio. Non sa che bisogna dividersi prima. I soldati ci portano via da soli, uno per volta. Anche noi raccogliamo le nostre stelle cadute una per volta; galleggiano nelle vasche dei contadini che le serve portano sulle colline per svuotare. Abbiamo scoperto le leggende intagliate dentro la morbida tessatura nascosta sotto le loro vesti. Non sanno leggere però. Poi i nostri occhi si buttano, affondati in pozzanghere, intolleranti d'ogni abbagliante verità, immersi nell'oblio. Disturbano anche il mio sonno. Alle quattro di mattina il mare esce dalla stanza e trabocca su questa pagina senza che lo spazio bianco sia disturbato. Parla piano. Siamo innamorati per un attimo e poi i nostri fidanzati ci premono fra le loro palpebre ed il buon senso delle consuete conversazioni. Puliti puliti facciamo i buoni bambini e lasciamo stare quegli sguardi terrificanti nello specchio. Procediamo attraverso le parole che scambiamo l'una con l'altra, stanchi della nostra realtà, noiosi come ragni. Più tardi il vento ci spaccherà in due. Prima o poi. Afferriamo alle fiabe anche se sono sempre uguali ed uguali anche le delusioni che si trovano lí dentro. Sei tu il momento vivace, lontano, quando il gatto prende la preda in bocca e corre via. Sei tu la stella più pura nel profondo nel cesso bronzeo dei burini. Però ti sei salvata ripensandoci sopra. Ti vedo un po' stanca in questi giorni sonnolenti.

9/22/1993
Manhattan

VEGLIA

Aspetto l'illuminante succedere delle ore pre-mattutine, purtroppo sempre più distanti da me in questi tempi. Anche oggi. Sbadiglio. Immagino, ancora una volta, la lontananza delle mie ragioni. Non mi devi dar retta. Ti volevo dire soltanto due parole sull'annegata verità di quella voce sonnolente, usando il dolce tono dei sogni che non potresti mai ricordare. Poi, la bomba mi è esplosa in faccia; le parole sono traboccate dalla diga della mia adolescenza. Qui uno tiene il controllo di se stesso. Qui si ragiona sempre. L'aquila ha finito di viaggiare verso ovest, in concordanza con i cieli, ed è finita qui, in questo bar. Resta là, fra i video giochi e il vecchio flipper. Non c'è più nessun mondo che ha bisogno del nostro potere di reggere, rimane solo l'insonnia, le bevande esotiche, l'aspettare per il mondo nuovo, e poi il conto. (C'è sempre il conto.) Queste città industriali non sono che sale d'attesa. Le stelle restano dipinte sul soffitto e non si muovono più. Siamo macchiati quaggiù, e orgogliosi del fatto. Apprezziamo specialmente la storia che abbiamo rubato ai nostri nemici. Li abbiamo coperti mitemente con sudari Cristiani. Non fu facile—non fu bello nemmeno—però, abbiamo salvato il mondo anche per loro, non è vero? Abbiamo salvata questa gentaccia miserabile grazie alle immagini che presentiamo del loro passato. Sai che la storia è sempre stata sacra? Anche i contadini e le serve sono felici, qualche volta, dopo che sono stati svuotati i cessi, non lo sai? Che altro ti potrebbe mancare se non l'atteggiamento giusto verso queste notti senza sonno?

9/23/1993
Brooklyn

POEM / WORDS (Unfinished)

caught up in time, housebound, kept from sleep
all night over manuscripts of upended prose;
escaped to the bar, overdressed for my poet's
nocturnal pose, clouded orange sop of a moon
looms above alphabet city, shitty luck
my *insomnium tremens*, burnt umber mood
softens to Sienna with a Brooklyn Brown
and drawn nervousness cigarettes w/ dollar ales
cupped
in bitter palms, naypalms to my academic
deep freeze: what the fuck makes my brain work?

The guitar grind perhaps? Drum thump of searing
shears? Offer appliances to the night, lovers'
friend,
'gainst the grain it rubs roughly, never happy
with any plot twist no matter how it eases
or turns from gray to red, reads, or pretends
to work. How does it go?

                              Like thus,
another Anglo-Saxon dream-vision:
"I awake. I am lying peacefully. I am an American
artist. I see pleasure I feel pain
and I have no guilt."[*]
                    i don't need to have. W/out running
i'm nothing talked about, rock 'n' roll ghost
even before the band split up. Drop. What note
brought down the walls; other mighty fallen ruins?
Volney blind before Damascus re-imagines his own
history.

Troy was a wave, shocked some sleeping poets
to epos—and tragedy was never far behind
the mystical words at Eluesis bridging night
with day when you can see the whites and the
blacks
of their eyes. Don't shoot! Saving bullets
scores, goes better than three for four,
dreams the waking world away.

---

[*] Patti Smith, "Babelogue."

                                    insomniac!
thy name is reader, frailty recovers lost
etymologies and whispers the poem back at me
through centuries filled with war and the absence
of the gods. Thus a curse is visited on the
children
of New Amsterdam, here, in the already aging new
world.
Tho' Seneca's appeal is still more than that;
it's this poetic efficiency 'at corrupts all
governing
and exposes one's heart to the four winds.
And we wind down,

                                        upbraiding
Zephirus for a song. Beer is for singing drunk
the music of the spheres in Boethius' ear
as he dies, content to be apolitical
at the last—we probably learned too late
lost, too, in so much metric economics—

                        not the poetic line,
however, the heroic nevermore of Blake's black
rhymes. Is the name the consequence of the thing
after all? Is my soul still on the auctioneer's
block
and sold for a secret? Gold was five times lead;
five drafts, the thought worded over five times,
five times thought to be holy, my quintessence
is this: that i can't stop wearing thin
in love's grip-maybe too late
                        to save my Dantesque p.o.v.

sorry, love
        i so wanted ever to be whole
and wholly yours but my stumbling lip; up popped
the devil, having heard, and he took my soul away
                                        maybe.

        3/30/1994
        Life Café, NYC

FIRST LIGHT (On the Lower East Side)

(for M. E.)

Amber shadows shouldering old rememberers' lost songs sold for beers and memories some long slow tolling's goal ago when I saw my hand write you over. That was all stolen then, in the leathery scent of tense longing and all the haloes that pain laid like palm leaves into our bohemian hands. The behemoth wish to lose this tune for a listener goes away now in the quiet show I'm watching in my own melancholy and fear.

Turn the page, washing blue and gaping in the ruts and up onto the reefs of things to do tomorrow, forgetting again the grins and derisions of this now. This now is screaming, too, enamored of its own remembering. Twilight beers in the glass brick glow of the Marz Bar take me upstairs to Vesuvio's where I mapped the sensate world in loud pages of love — and cupping faith in a sculptor's scarred palms, I let that liquid world seep into my shriveled fingers while the rest went down the drain with the bathwater.

We all live through others' vile laws, act and are acted upon, player pianos whispering in the arctic draft of fate and, simply, the way things are done here. But Anchor Steam and Rolling Rock kept us running in place, asleep in each other's beds but certain that affection and affectation's faked fashion would be crushed in our embrace. 'Cause we made stories happen upon their split personalities and they resented it when the climaxes caught up with them... didn't we?

5/30/1996
NYC

Autonomy Lost
(Anarchism Explained!)

I

It won't be difficult to follow me,
   the restless poet
      of Eighth Avenue
      ("il poeta della Baggina,")*
through streets of white sheets
of wind-blown snow
     over borders
'n' laborious landlords' billets
      blowing hard but never brooding
      never staying long enough in places
         to loom over disasters
         or entangle his all-stars' laces
         in repetitious lamentations
of past appointments kept and disappointments
skipped…

He hies instead
down alleyways 'twixt brick membranes
     exploring
         ,abandoned buildings,
from above: a grid, airy utopias borne aloft;

---

* Fabrizio De Andrè, "La domenica delle salme."

a *mappamundo* con-
crete continuum;
  an investor's homestead of applicants;
      seeds sown;
flats on their backs
    never called home;
    the lease we could do
      yearly.

He trips he tumbles
    leaping green trash-recyclables
    from out the snowplow piles
      a lush
life luring the low life back
to sleepy east side ease;
  (oh, sweet Bohemia
  tucked up tight in tenement heaven)

      but no!
    he does not sleep, he rather
    breathes wreathes of black smoke,
his own iron ire aimed at love's intricacies
'n' his tangled tangents of ideology;
    his body's betrayal of white-bread in the bone
        ,crumbs crumbling,
    he drinks a draught off
the ouzo bottle in which Manhattan floats
and moves off happily towards the lunch counter of his
dreams,
    his pen itching to scratch out all our hypocrisies
            in the Bonbonniere diner.

My illustrious cousin and i,
Fausto Festino, free citizens via our civil hands,
  (packing heat)
  plastered the streets
with anarchist propaganda 'til dawn,
   shunned our own unholy acts
  and saw the monkey's polka besides!
  (so many times!)
Years later, for instance, in a barrage of post-
apocalyptic flags
  on TV screen news services, at CNN
  at seven — film at eleven;

for something drastic has changed
 between the composition of this
  masked marauder of the poetic line
and today's post-millennial America, hence
this protracted love-song 'n' its provisional re-
inscription
   of facts
   of thoughts;
  the poet older now, the city
  younger, or at least less
  experienced; frightened perhaps
of its missing shadows, its Ellis Island-forged
strength and all manner of iron-ore immigration
immured itself out on the street, in on the date.

   On, therefore, down all manner of avenue
to our industrious seventh heaven
then, a bit of song we were seeking, sung
   to an old familial tune
with all new choreography. The Greeks

were gone so long
ago, really gone.

But *epos*, my lad, rears its meandering head and dons
its maundering shoes
        ,even here, in order
    to stalk nameless streets 'tween numbered
avenues of no declared identity. The emptiness
of *epos* is its key, the giveaway, its lack of a hero its
modernity.

Eighth Avenue might seem to you a dismal place to
practice poetry
Remarkable in its generic effrontery
        on an unremarkable isle
        where nobody ever says, "I do"
sublimely mine today and, as such, beautiful.

        But i did, do, have to have streets
because my hearth belongs to mommy, the landlady
        got the paper on me, the loving leaseholder
                        — you can't trust her,
though, to love you forever 'cause a scribe is so much
better
        at love
        in writing
    always building bridges ahead or behind
    the mill of his redirected memories — you can't know
    that dwarf, our evil and feeble blunders
        of innocent affection —
        an effervescence
eventually bubbling itself up, up, and away.

We should-a been-a Casanova or a Valentino
        ,anarchists of the heart,
    or at least their poetic "i"s.
        Instead we rented
        ancient dog-eared tenements
    ,were largely cowards before the law,
            against the wall, rowed
boats in Central Park, drank cocktails on the dock,
    watched the rulers rule
                with good will and ill.

Then it was Sunday
    and they tried to give us a day off.

Instead, this poet is trudging over sleep-filled piles of
shoveled snow, black
                as his heart, black as his lung;
    Pancia verso ovest, ed ecco! we arrive far enough
    back
    in time to leave
        the telling of our history, our
                most private oppressions, our
                self-accusations even,
    to collaborators' apologetic memoirs
            to talk about or not—a mamarama indeed!
                    (Why did i always fall
    for such pedophilic women? their giving birth
                a kind of masturbation?)

            i will have the leisure, though, to let it rot—a
            bone

to all those swimmers breaking winter ice
            accidentally brave
        titanically challenged by
            clumps of Eighth Avenue.

        Evviva Eighth Avenue!

Once bombs went off in basement apartments when we
invoked our love
            'n' carried our hearts
        in precious silver chalices to market,
        spent the soldier's queen of hearts,
        the jack o' diamonds; all other poets'
heads buried in basil pots, in medieval scriptoria,
or floating down the Hebrus happily-ever after.

        We thought but words
        — singing her name again three times in
        succession:
            "Eurydice! Eurydice! Eurydice!" —
            "drank but whiskey
        and borrowed but money"
            back in a lonely place
too lonely to be able to think but what happened
        surely happened, for we have written it
        and it was never so sweet as when
        we happened to pen the coming of the alternative
        to Christ.

As humble and ordinary as Eighth Avenue
        shoveled up in grime-collecting snow
                    —a turquoise February sun—
    my heart of hearts becomes again
        this long-suffering persona
                come home at last
in quasi-total identification with a splinter
        of some other, unnamed America
            (Eighth Avenue!):
                More liquor stores than banks,
                God's Lighthouse's dim windows
                and the precious Bonbonniere
        ,thick in steam and butter, its cat in my lap
                whilst i's eat.
    i'm caught again stalking my own poetic back
            doggin' my own self around
out the mistranslated bath houses, the old folk's homes,
i once owned
the bars and them think tanks:

        the avenue always seemed to
        expose the lie that we call "home"
                —where the hearth and hatred always hide.
Or is it simply
    that i dared to love Eighth Avenue more than i was
    ever able
to love you,
        Evelyn?

II

Sincere starts and fits
   fears and gifts
   the strange silence of the smoky diner
      when i write, words like:
"we're not parted
      until you drive that wedge
      between my shoulder blades,
      our ribs, 'n' hearteries."
      i'm supposed to buy you now,
         things?

But i preferred throwing bricks through yr windows while you sat at yr computer third drafting the Grrrl revolution, and in this i was proud, even then, to be wrong and alone, out of time, lucky enough to have fooled the gunners, as always.

i then gripped my own hand backwards—
      that one organ Dworkin

never counted on being un-
     naturally pacifistic;
only love was the bomb
     i lobbed
in your direction, bold as the axis
of the cross upon which they nailed that life-fucker
Iesu.

Then the Anarchist Poet of Eighth Avenue spied the Ice Princess in Washington Square Park. All dressed in black, a cigarette pout—it's hard, but not impossible—her feet propped on an ageless pile of re-frozen New York City snow, her butt cooling the historically green benches of all Manhattan folklore and NYC mythology of lost glances recounted by pouting poets all of their lurid lunch hours' exposed.

    (i *was* impressed!)

    But, no, the poet of Eighth Avenue speaks to no one—sees only to the telling of the tale being told, euphoric in his sidelong glances at such insufficiently symbolic figures.

In this state he flies
    with birds perceived outside diner windows,
the cigarette sliding
    through his head
    and out the other side.

My elongated sister
    ,uneven verse,
writes lines i might have
      otherwise dreaded:
  i do fear

"or eles mot I die"
Tithone's concubine
    time
    that built these citadels,
lies she tells herself
  — a rape in every word —
or Ed's eloquent cock in verse
    and prose,
      ashes on a paper plate;
      we may never
      be reborn — at this rate.

Our will is not strong enough
  — 'tho i don't know that really.
The landlady of my heart devises love a license
  ,equalizes me,
  ekes it outta me
  ,my ordinariness,
each and every day-e-ay.

The sun comes through the clouds now —
    still, i would have
    a word
    with the night.

This is the night
    all promises are fulfilled.
This is the night
    the flesh is made word.
This is the night
    we put ashes on our foreheads.
This is the night
    when somebody, somewhere, turns on the
    streetlights.

Then the Ice Princess lifts the lid off of the sky
    — what a prophesy! —
      and we die from the light
         of knowing, finally,
      what we should have known
all along: it didn't happen fast enough / i ate too
          much / other eyes have had me / i was late
          again / Babel rose, literally, overnight /
          i kept quiet to avoid a fight.

     Tight as it might seem
      "love" is the last word…
the lightest passion/medallion the body carries
through
every crooked street straightened out at progress' last
stop
on the road to the heart stop at the stair step to the stars
nor will the dead ever come back, despite sleep's
vigilant longing for them
as if it were already all gone in
      daybreak's luminous lament for the night

      and i may not love you anymore
         tomorrow. i will
    bury my heart once again at the crossroads
where the plodding of pilgrims protects it
         from grave robbers seeking souls
to enslave in porcelain jars and zombie dust.

How dare i say such things,
     or anyone. Ever.

i left my hat
on Eighth Avenue;

> i will unfurl
> myself for Decoration Day
> ,only a dime-a-dozen tipsy Manhattan
> barfly,
> the glorious result
of shame/guilt/surrender/abuse and my inane inbred
perversity
> to fail (or even to cross the street)

— it never even occurred to me to lick
> the melting ice from Miss Princess' encrusted
> boot.

Captain Anarchy
cannot explain: these thin lips' ability to kiss,
> the lack of straight lines
> in nature's bag of tricks.

Is justice willing to
cut up the world for yr kiss?
One time, the lights went out
> and
> i saw the phosphorescence of my own desire
upwelling in your eyes and flooding o'er
the floorboards, proving at last that
> the world is a hard, hard place
> to hoe a row
> to be beholden to hoeing
> your row
> and knowing that all of your suff'ring comes

from desire, not to suffer more
desire, source of all joy
     and why this euphoric poetic ghost — beyond
     the veil,
     inhuman — haunts Eighth Avenue in the first
     place.

O, ecstasy of anonymity!

    Evviva that Eight Avenue i once trod
while here the slave you crave
gave up his wiles for your smile.
    The love i tried to save got given away.
       i am the all you hate; (wait!)
        the good, the bad, and the shady
(every angel demurs to the sanctity of the human
side of the saint)
,all my every act aches simply to prove all your
science wrong
        ,Horatio,
your heaven, your earth, your row hoeing
   lox, stocks, bonds, and pork barrels,
       (see Saint Mark in Islam)
banks and all manner of official partition-bound
slavery;
         silver print etchings in authentic showrooms
           all throughout Soho
             so damn many abandoned realities
  in the mirrors of eight million subjectivities
         still,
    we're only just getting by.

Why is that? Why has art
not yet saved the world? Or
   has it?
   Already?
Unnoticed, set our hearts a-beating?

The words inscribed in your diary have left me
     dead and bleeding
       my meaning onto the bare tile,
words real as cash, diluting rather than increasing
     the knowledge of the world.
        (Years later
you publish just such subjectivities — preemptive
revenge
    on your own newborn son
      and his unfortunate gender.)

i only fabulate in the service of chaos
   at the behest of art
,*ad manos imos*, as always,
   dead and buried (in words
     but never inwards).

III

Later: below all such numbers, one snowlessly melting eve still
     inside Alphabet City limits (my reputable culture
     bunker)
on the outskirts of losing all such blue comforts
to the myopic waitress (surely she's right-handed!)
   my Octavian poetic i rides again(!)
    ,liminally, liminally,
nestles into a windy bar, 'n' then, when fatso comes back:
     she eyes the turn of my phrase, the
       scratch of my quill, the
       cut of my nonconformist jib
until her boyfriend sits back down at their mediocre table
     and she returns to musing upon the size of a virile
     member
         — it's so much harder in coupledom,
          being had in clubland.

My Lady Word i must have betrayed thee, destroyed
          even the simplest phrases, mumbled back
          at
          my teachers of rhetoric, lonely without
enough solitude, having fucked up
          the vertical hold
when the tints and the hues were pink and green and
the focus suspect.

All this i am is other now, out to lunch, come from
outside of me at some point, placed
     crookedly in a melting-pot, city;
          American anarchy
of misplaced avenues of no consequence
          evidently economically exploited democracies
                    of the heart,
          representative electoral colleges of repression
                    of the mind politic
                         schooled at the university of hard knocks,
a slippery shift between slavery and strike
          — ing it rich.

                    What a bitch.
To grow up here and land on all fours
          on Eighth Avenue, a poet
                    to boot.
And boot me they do, toodle-loo, toodle-loo.

It's the anarchy i don't do
          that i regret.
(and why i love the chaotic calm that Eighth Avenue is
so.)

But this, our balancing act, our
        daily, grim
menace of fact
    across imagination's lack of decorum
or diction—as in darting madly through traffic,
        avenue after
        avenue, through
venues where dandies laugh in swarms of winter sun
            in sum,
through all tomorrow's parties, the poet forced
to depart for ports perilous in search of beer
and solitude in alphabet city. The word "compromise"
springs to mind—Eighth Avenue itself
an image of actually interacting
    as opposed to signing up, contracting
    relations—preemptive strikes of the pen
        codifying hearts that yearn to beat
        as one.

    The blot on my conscience
        ,my lot in the world,
is that
    i will never own
        nor anything yours;
    no heap of stones, no pillory,
nor sinister pyramid enchanting the sun's rays to shine
        'twixt the sand dunes
        and camel dung. (Ah, history!)

    NO SACRIFICE!

However, the mother tongue
undone, in her own words,
    through peals of serious
speechifying—no niceties
spared the lash. Spins are now spun by not spinning
    —or more rightly, by simply saying
        one lives in a no spin zone—
the bastard right tramples the lilies
    of the field
    in Christ's name.
But the language of Eighth Avenue (and its
spokesman) is pure
    in its pre-Babelian mélange, still racing
to make sense of the world without
    exploiting the weary air we breathe,
        car exhaust and cloves, cigarettes and
        skunkweed.

    Therefore, to define the abashed rigidity of
canonical
        love—it faltered once
then renewed itself in some solemn dreams
        of all of its droning worker bees,
    their colors
        flying
        in the *TV Guide*.

Sirens wailing—as seductresses are wont to do, dying
and washing ashore—the Partenopean city has long
since absorbed their song:
their blood has painted its streets pink and alive—so
like the Lower East Side,

strolling through the cosmos of its streets, words
spoken to Aquinas
—what wouldst thou have of me for thy labors,
Tommaso?
—none but thee, words, none but thee
     …and the freedom to speak them.

          …and the world broke out in a rash
     of poverty and *immonezza*, Olé!

Love is dead, long live
love! Courtly love
is dead, long live lovers! Lyric
love is dead, long live
love! Psychological, blind
love is dead: long live
improvisational love!
          (We'll have to make it up
               as we go along.)

Eighth Avenue will ring
     with our stories then
on that exalted holiday of holidays
—on Psalm Sunday—when the poets sing the streets
and the tenements are filled with otherness and
     an alien America,
     an inconsequential America to come,
(and i knows it's coming)
     in which no one's vote matters anymore
     and where no one's president backs no one's
agenda, the banks will erupt and corporate,
international America

will ride off into the sunset
          bareback
naked, tarred and feathered, ludicrous
as it was to begin with.
          (Mouthwash!   Madison   Avenue!   Whitening
          powder!
          Dr. Suggs! Dr. Scholls! Dr. Pepper!)

On that glorious holiday
          Eighth Avenue will stop
               its bustle
     —cabs and hawkers, backfiring and honks,
     cops and keepers, sweepers and slaves
     busses and bustles, garments and karma—

On that holiday of holidays
     our phosphorescent assholes will hail
          the coming of the night
     and we will finally see the stars
          (without our prison stripes)
               and understand
     their totally useless existence—just like
               us all, each and every
     one. Sharing the darkness of the night
          (which allows them—and us—to shine!)
               in the spirit
               of compromise.

          First suspended 3/22/1994
          New York City

SOJOURNER (Back in NYC)

You arrive and it's spring, windy and green, and the fever keeps you warm and sweating into it, without sleep. Living on fear and wonder and the freedom of not having to care about sleep for a day or two. You're feeling strong after all that pain, but a little lost in all this familiarity. It seems long ago now that you belonged here and were always suspicious of its hold on you. Like sleep itself, you wake up in a strange bed and then remember, slowly, opening your eyes, that they're all strange now, now that your link to sleep has been laid this slack.

You're a tetherball, you decide, chipped off the knuckles, waiting to be brought down by gravity, heedless of your tether yet locked into an orbit for obscure reasons. Did it ever matter? Sleep? Its locale? Your partner in it? Was it ever anything other than a frame for the mirror holding your reflection, your various self-constructions? A nest in which you hatch yourself and from which you then fly?

You suppose you've come here for this: for the memory of so many constructive reflections, for the professional good cheer. Because sometimes you can only find the mirror by tracing the way its frame outlines the oblivion that may otherwise be divided solely by the gray border between sleeping and waking.

All these people passing, wanting to be admired without being looked at, without being seen.

* * *

It's different because your native defensive hostility's gone now, calmed by that European lack of liberty's kick-ass rhetoric that makes people laugh instead of scream at their neighbors. All those things done in desperation that should have been done in jest. So your old friends chip away at you, happy to see that innocent need of re-instruction in your eyes as they needle you into sync with their own disappointments, which they've already termed tragedies, until they tap the universal vein of sorrow and can welcome you into the sacred circle of suffering, either as an enemy or as a friend that they can resent as not as pitiful—or as deserving of pity—as they themselves. It would seem that they hate loved ones and strangers equally as they taunt us with their need to step on our toes harder and harder to make sure that we know that they're there.

There was never any doubt. Only they're taking tragic pleasure, now, in the comradeship of our resigned groans.

* * *

And love is somehow more real sunk within the pause, in the somnambulism, without an accepted rhetoric or a pillow on which to rest its head. Love is the secret behind all coming and going. No amount of staring turns it out.

*   *   *

You begin losing things, getting confused; wandering in the streets you so often trod with purpose before. That was another of your nine lives, you decide, when your home was in another person, when you weren't just visiting. It's that easy to get locked out, to forget your borrowed keys, to have to kill a whole night with coffee and cigarettes — if you can find a place to smoke them.

It's easy to blunder permanently into an uninvited acquaintance with one of these places of transit: a hallway in which you wait, a stoop upon which you sit, the greasy spaces of the grill behind the counter at Veselka Café. And, when you come to know these spaces, their resilience is astounding, their independence above and beyond our hurried passing, and we find their apparent consternation with movement of any kind disconcerting at best.

Two goodfellows pass, talking about time: a specific time that had been confused for the same time of another day, or an a.m. exchanged for the same hour p.m. You'd think, listening to them, that clarification could always be that simple, before or after the brightest moment of the day or the darkest moment of the night, a specific point on a discrete scale demarcating all of the incremental differences of the same proceedings. But our loves, our homes, their feelings and house keys, escape us. We wander familiar streets in a new daze, not looking for the things that we've mislaid but waiting for them not to matter anymore.

These are problems best solved with the solution of attempted indifference, committed deferral, a calculated ignorance of the situation's gravity. Nothing to be done but not doing—the wind will eventually unfurl the flags of our consciousness of its passing— and to wait for things to undo themselves, to loosen like the string that we knotted in our haste to get ready, not to be late.

* * *

Objects get in their way; those who look too hard and strut drunkenly through Veselka's on their way to the bathroom: counter stools, Sunday papers spilling off of tables, leaning mop handles. Objects are vindictive of those who, locked in to movement, believe themselves powerful. Objects invite us into the flow of the universe, demand attention, reflection and, ultimately, recognition. Perception alone isn't quick enough to protect us from all of the objects that we put in each other's way.

* * *

Distance collapses after four a.m. The fringes move in closer as the night slows down, and the losses loom larger and more irretrievable than ever, as the left hand of injury—or the recompense for the injuries that you have caused—begins to ache at your side. The sky turns blue, darkly, despite all of these predicaments, shifting locations and, finally, these scribbled locutions. Although one spends most of these transitory waiting-room hours praying for just this kind of symbolic event, they pass unremarkably and are only the tiniest twists in the unraveling of the knot. And knots are so easily tied, so easily bungled into when you're in a hurry and nervous.

*   *   *

But one comes back into time as well, always comes back into the here and now from out of the waiting room. That's the force of our construction of time. We always only digress, digress and return, return and stay. Sleep comes back with exhaustion and hunger, builds us a home as a haven against traveling, against lingering too long in the past, and all of the homes we've since been forced to vacate.

The trials of your distracted carelessness are almost over. You're walking toward the door now. You want all the doors to open for you; you'd like to open up the windows as well. Once again your dwelling is sleeping beside another human being—and though you were not wrong to have trusted in the past, now you are more trusting than ever, and this will assure the triumph of sleep over you, the rest you will need to be able to go on into strange lands again without being afraid.

5/1997
NYC

FINN BLOOD

"Remember, in Berlin?"

"Yes," peering up over the rim of her round glasses. "Of course."

It's cold in Helsinki, colder than he ever imagined. An eternal world of snow. "*Pakastaa,*" a Finn would say, "It's freezing cold," but, *jäädyttää*, he thinks instead, frozen, as in the food in the icebox. The third circle, he seems to remember, or was it the seventh? Strangely cold at the center, something to do with Satan's wings.

He raises and turns his head, looking for the calendar on the wall behind him, but his eyes only go as far as the window. The falling snow makes no sound. He thinks of the swirling atoms inside of all solid matter, of snow globes, of the illusion of the stillness of the snow-covered world. Worlds we do not make — we fall into them and integrate apparently. He would not have thought so at twenty. Learning languages had seemed more like a choice back then.

Because of that first time, in Berlin: he had led her out into the woods surrounding the art museum, intent on seduction. The brothers Grimm could hardly have done better. Despite a mild September chill and the rain-laden clouds, she had played along as he took off her clothes, piece by piece.

He'd been mostly in Italy, all through the summer before they had met, and then his money had started, noticeably, to run out in Vienna. *Jäädä*: to stay. He had decided to try to stay in Europe, no matter what. He was safe again now, past the risks of being in-between, in a home.

He marvels then, because he isn't thinking of time and place as two totally separate entities. Because to invoke Berlin is to think of its distance in train hours, is to imagine a future Berlin that they might again visit. The Berlin of their first meeting was still there, despite the years, also visitable, but in a different way. He wants to suggest they go. *Jättää*: to leave.

The wind kicks up now, the snow swirls around, and the trees outside the window shake their arms and fingers vigorously. He remembers reading the national poem, the *Kalevela*: "Whoever cut off a leafy twig," of the sacred oak tree "cut off everlasting love."

"Are you sure that it was an oak tree?" she had asked him, "because there are no wild oak trees in Finland. We have many *koivu*, birch trees I think they are called, *tuomi*, bird-cherry, and *pihlaja*, the rowan tree."

"Well, I read it in English, so maybe the translation wasn't so good."

He remembers the wedding section, the courtship of the girl of North farm, "Dark, sedgy farm." In order to win her, the hero, Ilmarinen, had three tasks to complete.

His eyes focus in closer, the distant snow blurs, and he becomes conscious of the solid drops of water falling down off of the eaves just in front of the window. A melting. He follows the drops downward and sees them jump apart on the cement driveway below—they will form a thin layer of ice by morning.

She's sitting across the table from him, lounging on the sofa, legs up, reading *Weird Tales from Northern Seas*—he translates from the spine. It's the Finnish translation of a Danish novelist's collection of Norwegian folk tales. She tells him that the book calls the Finns gann-Fins. "Gann," she explains, "comes from the Icelandic word *gandr*, meaning black magic." She grins, looking at him over her glasses and smiling. "We are the dangerous ones."

She goes back to reading, and he sees and studies the way the glasses magnify her round eyes and bring her closer. Her pronounced cheeks and round face above the spread open book.

"I am reading a story called 'Finn Blood.'"

Her hair is the oddest color, so red that it's actually orange. He'd assumed, when he had met her in Berlin in the mid-'80s, that it was some sort of new-wave dye job. Her eyebrows and pubic hair are brown. The first time he saw that was in Berlin, too, in the woods surrounding the museum. Pushing her panties down her white legs, past her knees, and off. The fall leaves also orange and brown in the dense woods all around the clearing, bending forward, his face in her lap, his tongue between the lips. "I want to," he'd had to say when she held his head in her hands and looked into his eyes.

"Why?"

"It's my favorite thing."

That was probably not the answer she had hoped to hear. She'd gone out on a summer vacation, and this American had followed her home, like a stray dog. "*Rakkaus*," she taught him, love. "*Rakkaani*," lover.

That red hair, those round cheeks. He's looking at her now; that smile she'd had then. She reads on, doesn't necessarily turn the page.

"Let's go through Berlin," he says, "on our trip; remember, we never did make it to the Bauhaus museum."

"This is true," she follows him again into English, which they are speaking together less and less lately, two of her fingers puckering the corner of a page. "Yes, all right; let's go back to Berlin. It will be fun."

Her cheeks are rounder with the smile then — the smile that he misses when it doesn't come — and he sees the lips that she makes bigger with lipstick. He remembers their first kisses in the dark woods, her holding back, holding his head in her hands and staring into his eyes like an animal — her glasses off there in the woods. Then, the lunging forward, the strong kisses, the biting. Looking up at the yellowing leaves of the trees above, her hands moving inside of his clothes. He'd wondered then if she weren't a little crazy — that look in her eyes, after all, as if she were going to tear into him to get at something inside.

Before the woods they had visited the Brücke Museum, walked the isles past the outlines of agonized and startled faces, the bright reds of Schmidt-Rotluff. They'd talked art; she talked art looking hard at his words through her glasses. He wondered if it was speaking English that made her concentrate so hard or was she really examining what he said. She was part of the *kulttuurikeskus*, the culture committee, back in Helsinki, she told him. The isles led them around the square museum and back to the entrance. They walked out into the briskly cooling early September air, the sky changing back and forth in the light wind, with their picnic.

"Do you think it will rain?"

"Maybe."

He had led her out into the woods.

"Do you remember the Brücke Museum?"

"Was it really the Brücke Museum? Well, never mind. It was as enjoyable anyhow, and the most fascinating thing in the museum were you."

"*Was* you," he corrects.

"Not subjunctive?"

"You seem pretty certain."

While putting her clothes back on she had told him, in the clearing, "I am a very proud one." She hadn't meant to do exactly this, he supposed. In a way, nor had he. All summer long in Rome, he had avoided other people mostly; he remembered then the couples lolling about on the dried summer grass in the Villa Borghese gardens where he went to read and proofread his morning's work in the languid July and August afternoons. Here there were fallen leaves already; he'd pulled her down onto the leaves, laughing, in an abandoned embrace.

Later the leaves were inside of his clothes; he had washed them off in the shower back at the youth hostel. (Before they'd left the woods it had started to drizzle.) Pulling the black stocking down her white legs, the panties past her knees, the scar on one knee he didn't notice then, her shoes still on.

"I don't want to make love to you here. I would miss you too much, then, after you were gone," she had said.

Now he remembers, Ilmarinen's first task: "To plow the adder infested field."

He closes his eyes when she begins re-telling him the story that she is reading, in a simplified Finnish that he can understand:

> A little boy, Eilert, plays with the little girl from the family of the gann-Finns against the wishes of his parents. Her long black hair and large eyes draw him in. He knows it is wrong to mix with the Finns; all of the villagers say so. His family competes with the Finn family for the fish in the bay. He steals corpse-mold from the grave of a Finn in the village church to atone for his crime of loving the little Finn girl. He spreads the corpse-mold onto his father's fishing lines and everything returns to normal. His family catches many fish.

Screwy logic, he tells himself on the train. And her hair really was naturally that color red, orange, whatever. They had wondered together—then, back in Berlin, having a beer in the hostel pub, after finally gathering up the courage to introduce themselves—why the whole world called it Finland when the people who came from there called it Suomi. Apparently it was the Swedish translation: *suo*, bog; *maa*, land; bog-land, fen-land. It had taken them a long time to remember to look it up for they had been busy getting settled. *Suomalainen*, one who comes from the land of the bogs, a Finn. She had been so occupied that winter with her exams (her eyes bent down toward the papers on the desk, hidden behind the glasses tilted across her bowed forehead), and he had conscientiously applied himself to learning how to teach youngsters English in order to help out with the money. Her university scholarship had kept them afloat, barely. They had waited for the spring thaw and the opportunity to travel again. *Sulaa*, he had learned by then, to thaw.

That had come back to him in the train, her screwy logic for not letting them make love in the woods that fall day in Berlin. *Syksy*, autumn. *Sykskuu*, the autumn-moon, September. She had to be back in Helsinki by October, *Lokakuu*, he now knew, the mud-moon. He hadn't been quite out of money, but at the point of spending his airfare back to the States if he stayed on any longer. He had gone on to Prague, to Berlin. Then he followed her to Amsterdam, to London, and home to Helsinki. That had not been screwy logic, because it had never been a logical decision on his part; he'd simply fallen into it.

"I was born in a city called Oulu," she told him in the hostel bar, over beers. "It is by the sea. I have always lived by the sea."

"Me too. Someday you will have to come to San Francisco. I think you would like it there; it's very beautiful."

Now she's sleeping across the seats in the train car, her head on his lap. The book she had been reading is propped against her thighs, her hand lightly upon it, a finger still marking the page she had been reading when she had laid her head down and closed her eyes. A body he knows now so very well.

"*Kultaseni*," she'd first called him—it had been the first word he'd learned. "*Ensimmäinen sana Suomea*," she taught him later, my first Finnish word. Now his thoughts often meander between the two languages, Finnish invading even his dreams, when he bothered to remember them, which wasn't often. Traveling, they were using English again, and it's like a novelty; they had begun using it in Copenhagen. She spoke German as well—how well he had no way of knowing—and would be taking care of the practical things in Berlin. He'd long forgotten his lousy high-school French, his sketchy start in Italian from the summer he'd spent in Rome. "*Unohtain*," he'd said once and she'd laughed.

"Where did you get that from? It is a really beautiful poem-form of the verb, to forget, meaning about: when forgetting everything at a certain special moment."

"Amnesia?" He'd wondered.

Olen unohtanut, he'd learned later, I forgot. *Minut on unohdettu*, I've been forgotten; as it seemed he had been, mostly, by his old San Francisco friends. The longer you are away the fewer letters you seem to receive and to write. Once it had been, "When are you coming home to visit? When do we get to meet this Finn with the flaming red hair?" But how many times can you ask?

Ulkomaalainen, outlander, foreigner—but in which direction, he wondered.

Then he remembers Ilmarinen's second task at North farm: "To bring death's boar, to bridle the wolf of the abode of the dead."

"Remember the youth hostel?" They'd looked at each other in the lobby for two days before speaking. Finally she'd just walked up to him—with those eyes!—and asked if he had a map. They'd made a date to go to see the Brücke Museum later that afternoon.

He remembers no first kiss, they were just suddenly together, holding hands as they walked to the bus stop, kissing as they walked through the woods around the museum, as if they'd been a couple for a long time. That was a funny way to think of it because, now, having been a couple for a long time meant that they didn't always hold hands or kiss as much as they once had. Still, he always craved her presence when she was not there. This body that he now knew so well, sleeping on his lap, her mouth a little open and breathing deeply.

"*Kultaseni,*" she called him, golden one. This body was his connection to the words: love/*rakkaus*. *Rakkaani*, my beloved.

"Do you remember the woods around the museum?" Picking up his coat, covered in leaves. The light rain beginning and their worrying if they'd make it back to the bus stop before it came a downpour. "I'd like at least to stay out the winter in Europe," he'd told her as they walked. He'd followed her to Amsterdam, followed her to London, and then she'd asked him to come back home with her to Helsinki. She lived in the university housing, but soon they had a room in a large shared flat, and later they were married, in front of her friends and family mostly.

"Yes, I remember the woods."

"I thought you were asleep."

"I was." She looks at him in that pause, without words, in which she just looks at him. Then she makes her eyebrows do a little jump. He'd always liked that, and she'd done it even then, in the woods, her head against the brown, the red, the yellow leaves. She had made her eyebrows jump, put her hand against the back of his head, and pulled him down until their lips were pressed together.

They had the train compartment to themselves all the way down from Rostock to Berlin:

> Eilert's boat gets capsized by the shark he is trying to catch. A grey corpse appears sitting on the other end of Eilert's upside-down boat as he hangs on for dear life. The corpse leads Eilert to the island of the gann-Finns, where the Finn girl takes him underwater to see her father who Eilert has offended but who is friendly and tells them tale after tale. These are the Finns in Eilert's dream that he has in the fever that he gets from being adrift in the cold of the North Sea. When he wakes, the Finn girl has been nursing him all along. When he wakes his dream has released him from caring what the villagers think and he is finally free to marry the Finn girl.

She had said then, walking through the woods surrounding the museum, "Do you think that this is the way back to the bus stop?"

"No," — he'd been wondering how much of what he said she could really understand. "No," he had said, "come on." They were well off of the path by now and coming upon the clearing.

"Do you remember this path?"

"Oh, yes: I remember everything." She remembers saying no, watching him and thinking, all the while, what they should do. She remembers the slow deciding to let him come home with her, the step-by-step building, then, of their home together. Her clearing out a space for him, for his work, and the hard work that she did to support them at first. He always called her, as he's first learned it in English, "My beautiful public prosecutor." Trying to describe what she did she had said, "You know the police force? I am the boss of them."

She wonders, now, about the balance between them. They had grown bored with Helsinki, but finally his work had begun to bring in some money, and they were free, this year, to do as they pleased.

In the clearing she touches him and asks, "Are you happy? In Helsinki, with me?"

He doesn't answer too quickly, either wondering why the question or thinking about how best to answer. "Yes. Yeah, of course. I don't think that I would have stayed if I hadn't been happy." Was that a lie? He wondered. Or a self-delusion? Few people have the will to buck inertia. Anyway, it didn't matter.

They come to what he remembers as the exact spot, and he lays his coat down on the ground, remembering Ilmarinen's third task. He remembers also that each task had been that much more difficult than the last and that he had been helped each time by the prize herself, the dark maid of North farm. "Catch the big scaly pike, the active fat fish / in the river of death's domain, in the lower reaches of the abode of the dead / without lifting a net, / without turning a landing net."

She stops him, holding his cheeks in her open palms and looking hard at him, smiling, as she had done the other time. Her eyes are grey-green, and she's opening them wide, making them as round as her cheeks. This is how she tells him that she loves him sometimes, when she wants to get around all of the impreciseness of their knowledge of the languages that they use to speak to each other. She does the thing with her eyebrows and they kiss. They lay down. Then, once again, he's pulling her black stockings down over her white legs, her panties over her knees and her curled toes. She pulls his pants down past his feet too. Their shoes are lying nearby, where they have kicked them off. They're blushing and giggling this time, feeling more self-conscious and less intense because of their age.

Afterward, when they're dressing, he says, "Let's go all the way down to Italy, even Sicily; you know, I've never been that far south. And I want to show you Rome, where I lived that summer just before we met."

"I think that we could spend this entire year away, traveling," she says, "perhaps go to your San Francisco, if you would like to, to be with your family for a while. Then the three of us can come home together next spring to Helsinki, so we will have left just as the melting has begun, and we will return to stay also just as the frozen season is over."

"*Kyllä, rakaani, palata,*" he says, thinking, "*palata,*" to return and, out of the blue, "*kotiin,*" home.

9/23/1986
Berlin-Copenhagen, in transit

SPRING REVISITED
(Artaud, Petronius, Bataille ...)

A rain of seed again
—Heliogabulus again—
well, sometimes, with a girl, i have wanted
to be the girl too for a while—
but now my phallus is blunted
by fatherhood, responsibility,
                    by time.

Tho' born a year too late
—or altogether too early—
we sexual specters ignore Jove's rain,
the phallic I, the skyscraper
the phallocentric pile-driving destruction
of every other way to mean.

                    But Heliogabulus' lesson won't
have me: i'm not viscous enough for Shiva,
tough enough for Nut, nor pussy enough
for Christ.

                    This is the story of the eye:
            —pissing on the eggs in the toilet bowl.
            —bicycles down a long straight street.

            5/8/2000
            Florence

THE SEIGE OF SAN MARCO

An event staving off its own message / each picture
begetting another on down the isle / a day's work /
done the humble meal / a fire at night / no doubt, in
winter / Savonarola's tears / on the pulpit to come //
Hiding behind the altar / he staves off the decision /
marks down the outlines / on down the isle / images
that return / "The same damn saint," says the
American turning away // They won't be able to
blame us for bullets / resting assured of some king of
kings / for whom they have voted / and all that
judgment crap // They hire / executioners all day long
/ up against these walls / each one with a paintbrush /
and then to sleep / in the simple cell // The making
and the undoing of the day and the night / stacked out
by the outhouse / grinding glass for the red
(bloodpaint) / soaking in the sin / to contain the sight,
they stare / looking into the sun / or hug the cross / in
blind faith //

6/26/1990
Florence

POMPEII ON THE PO

Broken bones. Broken bones and banks.

Streets long and narrow with poverty and spit. Spit spat up outta sore summer throats. Fever under a blackened sun. Perched on a porch in a plaster cast. Tequila—and broken bones.

Broken bones. Broken bones and banks.

Don't have a dime—or belief in. Fever. Sneezing up a sore summer throat. You want to scream through the broken glass that feels like your throat. Spit on your hands. Plaster, poverty, penalty.

Broken bones. Broken bones and banks.

Cities buried in ash. A TV pope and the clown of *Tangentopoli* sing "*padania*" for fun and profit. Oh, he's alive all right and spewing ash over a culture that gets in the way of his bank breaking, cash. Hands up! They break your bones in the back; you spit on the streets. You're afraid to talk through your shattered throat. Shoved down our. Fever-blackened sky. In plaster casts, centuries pass—still huddled by the sea, covering our faces with plaster hands.

Broken bones. Broken bones and the beat of the waves.

Waiting to escape. An ash-blackened sky tears at our eyes, tears at our throats. It tears at our hands. Your breath turns black, your back turns blue: beaten, despised—when the racists bank on a government backed by bankers.

Broken bones. Broken bones in ash.

Your sweat dries in the plaster cast.

3/13/1999
Amalfi

THE NEAPOLITAN *BEFANA*

Out from the swirling
sulfur of Mt. Vesuvius —
hairstyle 'Liberty,'
a cameo sealing a high-necked
nineteenth-century white blouse,
caught, at times, between Toledo
and Roma, French Bourbons
and Spanish Quarters, fat
Thomas poisoned with an egg,
unbroken, in a January mist
over the Tyrrhenian gulf,
— the Pizza Fairy rose up —
,more saintly than San Gennarí,
each of her ten knucklebones intact,
— and the huddled masses of plastic
garbage bags of Naples, of all shapes and colors,
gathered at her feet and knelt
in silent prayer.

    1/2011
    Naples

CATHOLIC WILL: A Perfect Roman Sojourn

Roman Fortune (innately
Mannerist) smites a curb-
    side tournament, its turn-
    stiles timed to mimic
land mines, whilst tragic
fame, mitred in disguise,
prizes suicidal maidens and
grants demijohns decisions —
                    to decant tanks, for favor,
                  to take arms against
                          a sea of turbines,

              which
by all rights should have been
shed by Fortinbras' cat,
              whilst
hopping over Roman bric-a-brac.

              However,
              tout court, our tongue
had strangled all our firm intent
and lent its charge to chance
    (said Cheshire to the waif)
of interactions all, both small and large.
Therefore, onward friction's
shoulders!   Bearing the boss
across the bridge of bad
humor (angels!)   to Papal precipices
'n' grumbling, placated

Tritons & Britons
in the rain, we trod on.

And just like that!
A spat!   Between
perfect strangers.

1/6/2010
Rome-Florence, in transit

IRRELEVANT IRREVERENCE

I

Descend from thy dimpled citadel and crouch down over humanity's—over history's—dung heap, disheveled Florentine citizenry of church, state, and village: both ye of the simple life and ye entitled warriors of race, class, and gender. You stormed that citadel only to find yourself Rapunzeled when the last rat jumped ship and ran, tonguing the idle taste of the crutch as you struck down republics in the name of humanism, art, and the church.

Your reasonable slumber awaits the coming of the tourists, the northern summer woulds, and the vituperative exchange of town and country in whose polemical mirror you see yourself refracted backward. You call upon your age-old self-same cobblestones, hobbling back into history (one—more—time) bassackwards in love with a fraudulent marble dwarf. Blemished martyrdom through the ideal defeat and the material victory, through xenophobia and self-loathing, the slow digestion of outsiders begins with bottle-shard crested walls.

You have to be right, you are written in stone.

II

Flowered fjord of born-again Balkans in this galleried gaol of picture postcards and discarded waves of curbside card players. The wayside here in St. Cock's Street where the cue winds down around the newspaper kiosk. Waiting for papers, With Out Papers, Italica turns inward on NATO's signal. One-two-three, drop! (People as debris.) The drowned Phoenician sailor washes up, Dante-wise, on the shore at San Gallo's galleria with another funny hat.

You are what you eat.

The faces of future restaurant proprietors — hereby cleansed of ethnicity in rice-paper wrappers. (People as shrapnel. One-two-three, drop!) — watch me as I pass, well below the tourist's water level. (People as paper to be filed and fitted, shorn and shouldered aside.)

Their quest is sidetracked here at the *questura* where unwanted guests endure the bravura of uniformed teenagers playing at social assessment, applying last year's perplexity to this year's platform, mutual consent a mute point. Beggars can't be snoozers, so steal a number and take a seat ... home. Maybe there's some hard labor your neighbors will let you do for them, if they're not too busy bombing your province of provenance.

10/21/1998
Florence

ASH WEDNESDAY

When it occurred to him that nearly everyone in this unreal city wore his or her mask voluntarily, he felt instantly better. There are no more illusions, after all, once you've realized that the dream in which you find yourself is only a dream. The realization, however, that the populace of the city's impression of reality was willfully false did little to alleviate the angst provoked by what those eerily frozen and brightly colored carnivalesque caricatures might be hiding, what the fleshy faces beneath the impenetrable expressions of innuendo and suspicion might be both concealing and, at the same time, exposing. The dream was indeed a nightmare, but nightmares — like all unpleasant events, trials, and tribulations, like life itself — also pass and eventually end.

*　　*　　*

I pushed the noble Montresor to his limit in the way of both injury and insult as a kind of social experiment. I wanted to see just how much abuse a Frenchman might withstand from a Venetian and then to see, once he arrived at his breaking point, exactly what manner of redress he would seek and how he would seek it. Such manias have been cultivated in us far back in time, at the lyceum particularly, but even earlier, with the subtle and obvious put-down, the practical joke, the special tortures that we reserve for our friends, for those closest to us. Having made a respectable hobby over the years of such pursuits (yes, I am the product of a life wasted in the enfolding arms of independent wealth), it was only natural that, on this, the very last day of carnival, I should dress in the bell-equipped and ragged motley of a clown, giving Montresor no sign of my intentions nor my careful observations of his reactions to my increasingly obvious provocations.

* * *

Although his dream-life continued in the masked, foreign city, carnival itself ended today. Arising out of its festive wake of strewn confetti and abandoned bits of costume, a memory overtook him of a carnival spent in Naples many years before, when he had met and spoken with his first Italian in her native tongue — or rather in the impersonal and power-laden *koiné* known as Italian. How many months of study had gone into that momentous occasion!

She had been a mere girl, Giusy; therefore, from the very first moment of his entrance into the foreign world that the new language appeared to offer him, its words had been eroticized. The next day, searching for his young Neapolitan acquaintance in order to speak with her a second time, he had encountered a friend of hers who, before taking him to Giusy, had asked him — as one did in grammar school — if he "liked" her. The question had puzzled our linguistic novice. How could such a thing be possible, be taken seriously, between him and the young woman when he could only feebly struggle through a few disconnected phrases that she were able to understand? Even if the speaking of these preciously few incomplete sentences were gestures of great courage and desire on his part, both for her comprehension and in order to bravely enter into another world.

*   *   *

Spying my victim across the crowded and festive piazza during the supreme madness of the final days of carnival, I elected to move in Montresor's direction, facing the other way, so that he might instigate our encounter himself if he were so inclined.

Indeed, as I had expected, he opened this round of our sparring with a salvo of stale and ill-concealed puns — how I was "luckily" met and how much the fool outfit suited me — little understanding the triple meaning of such jokes in the eyes of he who had actually engineered them.

He then began the inevitable attempt to entrap me that I had so long awaited.

One of Montresor's greatest conceits was his assumed French cultural superiority in wine expertise. Therefore, he chose to seek to ensnare my interest by announcing that he had managed to obtain (at the very peak of the carnival season!) what had been sold to him as a cask of genuine Amontillado — but that, rather than bothering me with the wine's authentication, he was on his way to have Luchesi taste and declare the presumed vintage's verity or falsity as an authentic Spanish sherry.

What a sad ploy it was. I forced him to play the ruse to the hilt, though, feigning drunkenness and repeating the word "Amontillado!" over and over again to see how far he would go to keep up the game. Verily, I wished to judge his level of commitment at this juncture of our *contrasto*. Finally, convinced that this was indeed the long awaited enacting of Montresor's revenge, I ridiculously declared that Luchesi, "cannot tell Amontillado from sherry." Stupefied that Montresor did not notice the idiocy of this statement, even after I made the outrageous blunder twice, I bad him lead on and, in a moment, we were aboard his gondola and making our way toward his family's usurped *palazzo* fronting upon the Grand Canal.

* * *

Many years later, during his divorce negotiations, his wife had proclaimed that they spoke two separate languages, but that the difference in their various methods of communication had nothing to do with either the English or the Italian language. However, like almost everything that she said, it had been an obfuscation of herself, another way of hiding her reasons and intentions. She, a true citizen of the city of masks, donned a smiling or frowning disguise over her actual face and its desires as the situation required. Regardless of her mastery of English or his of Italian — which Victoria, against all Italian regionalism, had adopted and actually spoke as her own tongue — their various perceptions of reality were linked to the rhetorical principles of their two native languages, his to an almost offensive nudity, practically an exhibitionism of experience and reaction to the world that allowed him a rich inner life of imagination, and her Salome-like seven-times-veiled rhetoric in which masks hid only other, deeper, and more subtle masks, disallowing her any inner substance other than secrets themselves, darkness, and a rather eerie absence of center beneath the frozen expression of her impeccably vacuous decorum. Victoria never displayed a fixed compass point, neither in her personality, her proclivities, nor her preferences — she exploited every situation to a momentary objective without scruple, logic, or any innate Italian sense of aestheticism either.

Such an intricate system of infinitely stacked and interchangeable disguises allows the native speaker of Italian to avoid all stable concepts of reality, all moral absolutes, any semblance of rule or order, any sense of loyalty; even attitudes or stable proclivities (such as a simple like or dislike), and certainly the illusion of any type of passion, vanish beneath the continually renewing stream of self-justifications that each costume argues for them. Every action becomes both crystal clear and muddied beyond recognition in the keen half-light of the excuse, the momentary self-justifying apology.

The utter inner emptiness of the protean city of self-justification made it both a political center and the constant butt of jokes throughout the rest of Italy: it rewrote not only the daily news but also its own history in an imaginary and self-absorbed polemic against itself.

Perhaps my experiment upon the limits of Montresor's sense of outrage and vengeful impulses strikes you as rather eccentric (to say the least), odd, or even suicidal — and so it was. I had long ago given up any claim upon this life. For some years I had acted more or less as if life itself were a somewhat inconsequential enterprise. For me the carnival was ended, and even the approaching springtime bore little promise of future amusements. Or perhaps it is more accurate to say that my life had become an unending and self-consuming revel, a kind of melancholy private joke.

I had chosen Montresor as my executioner in order to add a bit of sport, of game, of spice, if you will, to my inevitable demise — because I was too much of a coward to indulge myself in a sordid and mundane handmade suicide. Yes, I must here declare that I am indeed too frightened of physical agony to have indulged my penchant for self-destruction. I had never been able to get my hand to follow the desires of my brain in order to put the world away once and for all. Also, I must admit that a friendly acquaintance had laid a considerable sum of money — to be paid to my heirs, you understand — on the assertion that, "That deplorable and politic coward of a Frenchman Montresor would never be capable of harming even a gnat, no matter what the circumstances." It was a wager that I was, at that time, well disposed to undertake.

Perhaps you blanch to hear the unspeakable word "suicide" — and yet is not our entire religious edifice constructed upon the pedestal of its near cognate "sacrifice," and our political system shaded beneath the canopy of suicidal "heroism?" Why else the perennial popularity of the figure of the vampire? Because we feast upon blood the whole day through, my friend; because we revel in plain daylight at the spilling of blood, be it that of an enemy, a burnt offering, or even our own heroic or sacrificial wounding. We may hide the word behind a wall of subterranean silence or mask it in religious or political jargon, but blood, sacrifice, execution, and suicide are our culture's most common foodstuffs, its quotidian bread and butter.

Montresor would be my Judas, my pawn, my more courageous hand, as well as the instrument of my salvation — perhaps even his own. For, without sin how could he ever hope to know either repentance or salvation? In my own malicious and playful way, I had invited him into a mutually beneficent, if macabre, *pas de deux* of cosmic importance. I was offering him both the excitement of physical action as well as the metaphysical key to his own spiritual consummation. Out of the ashes of my murder, his star, too, would be able to rise, if he so desired, to the very right hand of our judge and savior in heaven.

*   *   *

Such reasoning — that every statement in the jargon of the above-mentioned city is phrased as an act of self-justification — assures that the final word of every utterance in the city's dialect will be "*capito*?" Since the meaning of every statement lies buried some six feet beneath the superficial words of its phrasing, because there is no idiom in the dialect of the city that means "at face value" or "plain as the nose on your face" — because even in the modern Italic *koiné* (based upon the dialect of the very urban center in which he found himself exiled), facial expressions have value only insomuch as they are able to manifest themselves as masks both disguising and therefore revealing subtler, more hidden meanings. Human faces, therefore, have ceased to have any substantive value in the city's self-expression except as the objects of aesthetic/erotic and reified presentations of a material nature. Consequently, most outward spoken or written expression here bears the unreality, the hyperbole, and the showmanship of the worst kind of pornography.

Because of all of these reasons, the finest rhetorical utterances emanating from the great humanist centers of Europe reek of a faked orgasm.

*　*　*

In this brief transit where the dreams cross, I willingly followed Montresor across the threshold of the oblivion that he has prepared for me. He had admirably disposed of his servants and the ancient *palazzo* that his ancestors had co-opted from an executed Venetian traitor echoed hollowly, endlessly, in its labyrinthine depths, as we entered into its foyer from the landing on the Grand Canal.

My host lit the tapers of a pair of candelabra in the great arched entrance hall, the rising tidal waters lapping up onto the steps at our feet in the wake of our gondola's landing. He handed me one and led the way, and we descended a narrow staircase into the cellars tucked beneath the *palazzo*, below the water level, deep into the bowels of the swampy lagoon in which my ancestors had taken refuge from a barbarian and war-torn Italy dominated by dukes and barons and their various mercenary armies, the backbone of the so-called Renaissance.

Knowing now that I would probably never return again to see the fog-shrouded and soggy daylight of my native city, I plunged into the bowels of the *palazzo* happily, immersing myself symbolically into the lagoon, plumbing the depths of the mother that had enfolded, protected, and then shriveled and rotted us all through our increasingly adapted amphibious skin. I was indeed elated to be so close to an actual rather than a simply *pro-forma* event, my courtly and mannered existence having become so disturbingly vapid and pointless to me.

Even though he remained somewhat passionless in his role as a vengeful executioner, I smiled upon Montresor's resolute shoulders as he led me toward the consummation of our jointly nefarious plan for my death, deeper and deeper into his own subterranean catacombs, between the casks, butts, and pipes of foreign and domestic vintages that his transposed French ancestors had mirthlessly gathered and stored here, more for ostentatious display than for pleasurable consumption.

Yes, the Montresor family had been a quiet and reluctant visitation upon our city for several generations, not unlike the Jews and other outcast *extracommunitari* that populate the more fetid of our swamp-islands and who throng among our already outcast, so-called native race in the marketplaces and public squares. Boccaccio claims that all of the vermin of Europe swirl into the vortex of Venice like shit into a draining cesspool, without understanding why we not only allow but invite them to do so — because, unlike the insulated and land-locked Tuscan, we know the unspeakable darkness inside of the right souls of the accepted and mannered courts of Florence, Rome, and Milan; of Vienna, Berlin, and Munich; of Warsaw, Prague, and Moscow; and even of Paris, London, and Madrid. Because — God help us — we cannot bare to stop them. We Venetians relish the truest form of society: our own secret accord with power, our unflinching sense of secret justice allows of no appeals and is, to us, the one true and just democracy in a chaotic world of mutual distrust.

I smiled, I say, at Montresor's sloped shoulders and impeccably erect carriage born of so many generations of pretending to understand what his kind could never really fathom — the Venetian soul in all of its perverse and unavowed triumph. I laughed at his pompous uncertainty and, seeking to hide my mirth, feigned a hacking cough.

The Frenchman immediately attributed my discomfiture to the chill and dampness of the niter lining the black and dripping walls of the artificial catacombs. More feeble jokes ensued, more false protestations of feigned concern, as well as the suggestion that we end the expedition at once.

But I, wary of his cowardice cheating me of my eventual triumph over his Christian soul, proclaimed, in order to give him more courage, "The cough is a mere nothing. It will not kill me. I will not die of a cough."

*   *   *

Many years before his divorce from Victoria, the girlfriend he had acquired while studying at the Italian university, warned him that, "If I ever find out that you're only going with me to learn Italian…" Had she been American, she probably would have read in his reaction to her prodding, in the startled expression on his face at her unuttered threat, that this was indeed the case—even if he himself had not been explicitly aware of the fact until she had spoken it. But she rather preferred to let the moment pass with her simple warning intact; not noticing (or pretending not to notice) how reflective and uncomfortable her admonition had made him.

Not long after this, however, he had fallen in love with her despite his lack of desire to do so. She had gotten under his skin more and more as their relationship progressed in time. However, even as she became increasingly adept at infuriating and pleasing him with her moods, jealousies, and affection, he still often thought, "Thank God I'm not in love with her. Heaven knows what she might make me do if I were in love with her."

The moment of the realization of his true feelings had come only because he had been forced to observe his own face's expression at the moment of their parting. He had climbed aboard the night train to Paris, leaving the woman, the city, and their language behind for who knew how long. He had hoisted his bags onto the couchette and gone to the window outside of which she stood on the platform below, smiling, tears streaming down her cheeks. Suddenly the train jerked, lurching forward in departure, and he had been confronted with the apparition of his own face reflected in the glass superimposed over hers.

The train began trotting forward, and Giulia's face detached itself from his own and moved, ever swifter, off into the growing enormity of the past. He had been left with his own image in the glass staring back at him, a detached face observing itself like two silent strangers alone in an empty *couchette*, each of him hovering like a ghost above the now swiftly tumbling landscape outside the window. He watched as the stranger in the glass watched his own features contort into the agonized grimace of one who had just bid farewell to his beloved and real tears began to squeeze from his eyes. He had been in love with her after all, despite everything, despite having had no desire to fall in love—he found himself suddenly washing up onto an arid beach, alone, slipping noisily through the night on his way toward a country that spoke neither of the two languages with which he had become familiar.

*   *   *

Montresor knocked the head off of a bottle of Medoc, and we shared a last *brindisi* together. I toasted, ironically, the corpses of his ancestors lining the walls around us, and he, also ironically, drank to my long life. We shared for a moment the brotherhood of assassins, an unbreakable bond of mutual self-contempt, and I grew certain that our destinies were now inexorably intertwined.

I felt what I imagined to be the comfort of such fellowship and the heady red wine warming me inside: interior embers glowing with the flames of alcohol and expectation. Still, I worried for his resolve in this matter in light of our newfound camaraderie. For, if we Venetians had ever once allowed any of these native foreigners into our vicious circle of cursed friendship, they would have instantly become our equals, equally obsequious fellow citizens of the *Serenissima*. Therefore, in order to recall him to his duty toward me, his avowed tormentor, I feigned forgetfulness and asked Montresor to remind me of his family's outdated and up to now purely symbolic coat of arms: a golden human foot crushing a green serpent whose fangs were well imbedded in the foot's heal, its poison no doubt already acting upon its victim, as was evident in the very action of the foot stomping upon its humble aggressor. *Nemo mi impune lacesit.* To leave off my assassination at this juncture of our adventure, after my invocation of his ancestors' credo of vengeance even at the cost of death by crushing, despite whatever yearning he might have had for integration and acceptance by Venetian society, would be a cowardly renunciation indeed.

Now that he was reminded of his family's honor before the very tombs of said ancestors, in all of the accusing and profound silence that the tomb inscribes into its marble monumentality, we were clear. What passion had instigated, I assured myself, duty would soon complete.

Even so, a moment later, as he continued to taunt me with the frigid air and the damp niter of the cellars, which were growing ever thicker around us as we descended, my own resolution faltered momentarily. Perhaps the experiment had gone far enough. Perhaps some wagers are better lost than won. Must I truly go through the agonizing and squalid death that Montresor had prepared for me — leaving aside the just or unjustness of the sentence — somewhere even deeper into these forlorn and forever foreign sepulchers lined with the bodies of dispossessed and disgruntled Frenchmen, wine casks, and lagoon-rot?

Presently we drank another draught of malmsey and, boisterously euphoric now — and even warmer at the pit of my person, nay, in my very soul — I again taunted the outcast with a Masonic gesture that I invented on the spot to further humiliate the pitiful, bungling foreigner and forever to brand him (even if only in his own mind) as a non-invitee to all of the sham secret societies and imagined brotherhoods of which I myself had grown so weary.

Deftly he produced a trowel from somewhere and actually completed a pun of his own devising.

At once his face transformed into my own, as the marionette cannot but take on the features of the puppeteer who manipulates its strings, and I realized at last, and utterly, the upshot of Montresor's plan. I rejoiced inside, the liquid fire in my heart glowing ever brighter, at the impending consummation of all of my long-engendered machinations.

"You jest!" I exclaimed in amazement, not having previously deemed him capable of such levity, nor especially of such wit.

*   *   *

No longer desiring any specific companion, even despite his great facility with their language, meant distraction on his part, distance from those around him, and ultimately resentment. Not to care for others soon comes to mean more than simple neglect. The buds of indifference bloom into the flowers of annoyance and then finally wither into an abject loathing. His wife's rejection of both himself and of the family that they had made together soon bore the fruit of alienation, a new secret duplicity at its core; her false abandonment — in reality her marginalization of him both physically and legally — made him an immigrant again and prompted, in him, a thinly hidden resentment that manifested itself in answer to the oddest and often most unexpected pretexts. While the theme of his complaints were always justice and how it had abused him, his disgust often fell upon seemingly innocuous objects such as distracted drivers, inconsiderate teenagers, thoughtless litterbugs, anyone, in fact, who got, ethically, in his way.

*   *   *

Eventually we arrived at the inmost core of the funereal pit beneath the *palazzo* and, true to form for the exile, the outcast, and the *émigré*, a reminder of the Montresor homeland bearing the features of a death's-head appeared before us; it looked something like a stage set. The innermost chamber of the *palazzo*'s subterranean strata, the *sanctum sanctorum* of the dispossessed family, had been modeled upon the catacombs of their beloved and forcefully abandoned Paris.

Bones lay stacked, not merely piled but arranged, designed, even sculpted in all manner of macabre filigree and arabesque upon the walls. The Montresors, a Huguenot family, had fled to Venice from a particularly Catholic period in French history and, upon arrival in their adopted city, had apparently begun to imitate — in secret of course — the very papist swine who had driven them from their homeland by aesthetically arranging the remains of their dead predecessors beneath their usurped Venetian manor. It was breathtakingly sublime in its appropriateness, its perversity, and as a suppressed sign of the family's longing not only for their homeland, but to be one with those who had persecuted, maligned, and eventually driven them from their very homes in the name of some Pope or other's infallibility. Despite a nominal conversion to the followers of Martin Luther, they had been unable to unlearn the macabre lessons of our Catholic obsessions with death and decoration.

The circle again appeared before me, complete.

I raised my now faltering candelabrum in order to better view the tomb-space that Montresor had prepared for me. The air at this depth was too foul, however, the oxygen in too short a supply, to allow the tapers to flare large enough to entirely illuminate the scene.

Oddly enough, despite the niter, the damp, the frightful cold, and the extra chill of the dominion of death surrounding us on all sides, pressing down upon us with all of the weight of the ill-abused and melancholy house of Montresor above our heads, I felt still — and even stronger than before — an ever-warming glow at the core of my being.

He bade me to proceed. I raised my hand near to the manacles hanging inside of the aperture and waited an interminable amount of time for him to finally jump up and shackle me to the spot.

*   *   *

It was not long before the skittish and inevitable people of the city began to gently inform him that, although he spoke their language well enough, he often said unutterable things in their breathy and sinuous version of the national *koiné*. As if the language had been devised as a trap for the unwary foreigner, it became clear to him by and by that many of the words that he had learned in their language, most discourses of any real substance were, in fact, taboo in actual conversation. Such words existed only to be passed over in silence, in order not to be spoken—not by him anyway.

For instance, one was apparently not allowed to express suffering but only protest, nor to display weakness outside of complaint, nor invoke fear except as outrage. One was not allowed to speak ill of those who did ill regardless of the verity of his or her claims because no one wanted their own self-serving or impulsive actions exposed or judged by others. Truth in speaking was, apparently, entirely beside the point; indeed, the language had long ago replaced the words "right" or "good" with the word "beautiful," ensuring that correctness lie in the beauty of the rhetoric of the argument rather than in the shifting chimera of any type of moral or ethical absolute rule. In a language of apology and self-justification, it becomes bad form to assign guilt to the actions of others. The heart of the city's experience of itself lay in its vocabulary of self-aggrandizement rather than in any talk of frailty, self-doubt, or, least of all, blame. In this city it is not for us to blame, but rather for others to explain away all amoral—or even pre- or meta-moral—human action and interaction via necessity and/or inevitability.

*   *   *

Nervously, Montresor laughed, embarrassed no doubt that his plan had come this far, jabbered some nonsense about having to leave me now as he uncovered the bricks and mortar that he had so carefully disguised beneath a pile of the bones of his ancestors, which would now serve to entomb me beneath their adopted home forever. The bones of such Frenchmen are only good for hiding the truth, I mused, for obfuscating all true intents, honest desires, and the cruel ingenuity necessary to bring such acts to fruition.

I was pleased with myself for having made a man of Montresor, to have separated him from these tawdry, obsequious, and silent exiles who had crept in to our midst, from an entire legacy of serpentine cowardice in the name of martyrdom.

"The Amontillado!" I commanded, now fully aware—as we both were—of the true meaning of the word, the deed that it had come to represent, lifting it like a new family crest to adorn the entrance to the secret and holy space that the mason was beginning to build around me, row upon row, with bricks and mortar, for my secretly inglorious enshrinement. My temple was to be constructed in an architecture of secretive and hideous murder, would be a room without windows or light, without means of ingress or escape, a secret space in its author's own mind and conscience, forever bearing the emblem of a cask of Amontillado.

The joy of his homage smoldered hotly within me. The wine that I had mistakenly thought to be lingering in my stomach was long evaporated, but the calefaction at the pit of my being rather waxed than waned as I presided approvingly over Montresor's labors. I daresay that I broke out into a long series of low moans not unlike those intoned by our most famous Venetian courtesans as they plied their profession of *amour* for lucre, feigning both pleasure as well as a pitiful lament for their lost honor for the benefit of dissipated nobles such as myself—then plying the trade of a far truer form of love in the field of versification in their leisure hours.

Perceiving at last, however, Montresor's discomfiture with my obviously pleasurable rapture and equally feigned lost honor, I managed to control my outward reactions and turned inward to contemplate the ardor growing in my bowels. I lapsed therefore into a long, obstinate silence. Long he labored, then, at my feet as I presided over his undertaking in contemplation of the heat growing inside of me—what was this spark being fanned, this veritable holocaust mounting in my belly and inflaming my entire torso? What did it mean to our *pas de deux*, to the *denouement* of our pre-arranged tryst, if indeed it were a significant effect of the experience?

Presently the intense calescence sent me back into throws of ecstasy, and I could not help writhing amongst my chains and bells and motley at its fiery urging. Although all that surrounded me was cold stone, the putrid niter, death, decay and the frigid dampness of the grave, I was sweating and agitated beyond endurance.

Then, for a time, I was again able to calm the throws of my burning joy and to remain silent as Montresor raised another three tiers of my sepulchral enclosure.

At last, again, wave-like, the embers glowing within me took air and re-ignited scorchingly, producing a number of screams out of me that filled the dreary cavern with an audible light, visibly shaking us both.

*   *   *

Being right, however, being just, was often of little consolation. He had railed against the city's masks for too long. It began to wear him out to protest so, only to be ignored and finally domesticated by the city and its citizens to the extent that his clamor became nothing more than another form of silence. His words themselves, spoken in all sincerity, were passed over by his listeners as no more than verbal masks such as they themselves were wont to wear. How could they interpret such words otherwise when the lascivious, fixed carnival grin was all that their language afforded them? It took him a long time to understand that the seemingly thoughtful listener was doing little more than formulating their next self-serving salvo when they appeared to be digesting the tortured utterances of his inmost thoughts and feelings. They were merely drawing the dark ashen cross upon his forehead and offering him the pious luxury of reneging upon himself and upon his own words for the greater good of silence and conformity to their *omertà*. The mask of the unspoken and the unheard reason is a kind of absolution for all human feeling and mutual participation in the act of becoming human.

*   *   *

At last the wall before me was completed except for the final stone to be fitted into the uppermost corner slot. Despite the intense candescence of my soul and body — indeed the very enclosure appeared now illuminated from the glow pouring forth from my body — I could not abstain from taunting Montresor one last time, to see if he really had the stomach to brand himself for ever with the mark of Cain.

My ebullience overcame me even as tears of joy hung from my cheekbones in peril of dropping to the flagstones of the tomb-chamber. "Ha! Ha! Ha!—he! he!—a very good joke indeed—an excellent jest. We will have many a rich laugh about it at the *palazzo*—he! he! he! —over our wine—he! he! he!"

"Amontillado!" he replied, as much as to say, "Death sentence!" and the significance of the word completed its transformation from signifying a mild form of sherry midway between the lighter *fino* and the darker *oloroso*—much like Montresor himself, tepid, neither wholly dark nor light, killer nor victim—to the most despicable of all sins: murder. Like the sherry he named, even though I had fortified him with yeast and alcohol, he would never live up to the true ironic darkness of my milieu, the practice of which I had made into a fine art for so many years.

I could stand his company no longer—I was fit to bursting from the searing light enveloping the enclosure that I had yet to understand. I now knew, however, how much I longed to feel it consume me utterly.

"He! he! he!" I laughed, "Yes, the Amontillado," as if it had all been his idea from the very beginning. "But is it not getting late?"—we had already heard the midnight bell toll the end of carnival and the advent of Ash Wednesday and of Lent some moments before— "Will they not be awaiting us at the *palazzo*, the Lady Fortunato and the rest? Let us be gone," I implored, the cell growing now painfully bright around me. I had become terrified lest he look in on me and see my apparent transformation—it was not an event that I would have shared willingly with any other human being.

Insipid as ever, instead of placing the final brick into place and leaving me to my solitude, Montresor repeated my plea to be quit of his troublesome presence — and that of the whole wide world as well: "Yes, let us be gone."

"For the love of God, Montresor!" I shrieked, the igniting chemicals within me taking over, transcendent, all-powerful, unbearable at the last. I was forced to halt the intake of my breath, to stave off any movement at all, until he should place the final brick into the wall if I wanted to count on his not turning back on his task even now. I could feel my flesh growing still warmer, desperately searching for the oxygen it needed in order to ignite and reduce me to a cinder — and still he delayed, calling my name, asking me to call off the execution, begging for the reprieve that I would never have granted him — and tossing his flambeau in at my feet in order to see what I was up to.

My body began to tremble in anticipation, and I nearly swooned from lack of oxygen when I heard him finally thrust the final brick into its place, and my ecstatic, writhing form, my useless husk of a body, drew in the fetid air at last and exploded into a pure blaze of spontaneous, transfigured, combustion.

Delapsus resurgam.

BEATRICE IN PURGATORY

All the will in the world
dwindles thin to this
returning thought: running
in place—now a weight to bear for
ever after, a feather to carry
,nary a flint to bury, but a
needle igniting the haystack 'n'
everything flammable burning to the ground.

Simple. Deceptive as a dream
etching roses in, funereal lilies along
light strands of resurrected memories
every time we were apart:
now a brighter gaze
envelops spheres both great and small.

Light itself waxes heavy
under all that sky
that doesn't dare reign
supreme, that
can't fight entropy, that can't
help falling into infinity: some
god's simultaneous expanse and collapse.

5/2000
S. Francesco

ROMANCE (an episodic narrative)

Escape a taut tourniquet bent
torment not to drip drop drip
that tension out, to congeal
the temptation to taste the deep
at the nape, bristle in time
to brush past perfume sick
or sweat lovely, B-L-A-R-E, trestle
past the other train, not on time
no, never kept intact that
ticking thought

         that wreck
that wrought this romance.

    10/2002
    S. Francesco

THE AMERICAN CEMETERY

"Tu n'as rien vu à Hiroshima, rien."
— Marguerite Duras

I have written and erased this opening sentence so many times now that I'm beginning to despair of ever putting anything down at all. At last I have decided to begin with a simple statement of identity, to let you know who is speaking and why he speaks in such a plain manner. I am a man of letters. I have decided upon this segment of my identity because it is true and because the pun that it makes is even truer. I am an administrator and an instructor of literature at an American university abroad. I was born in the United States.

As a sometimes teacher of literature, I'm well aware that the style of this text is rather bland. That is because I have never desired to write fiction, and, despite many years of studying the great writers of the past, I have never sought a style for my own thoughts other than what the words themselves led me to formulate in a classroom. I don't want to begin this with an apology in the modern sense, although I do feel a little like Socrates on trial for daring to put words down on paper at all.

Quite simply, I have been thinking a lot recently about the American Cemetery.

Every day on the way to work my train passes the American War Cemetery along the Arno River between the hamlet of Le Sieci and Girone, the little town nestled in the big circular eastward bend of the river just outside of Florence. I have had many thoughts as these daily trains that I take rattle around that bend, tilting uneasily into the Compiobbi station. (My wife says that it's as if the train were trying to tip us out there, roll us all down the hill, through the town, and into the river below.) The Compiobbi station is formed in the semicircular image of the Arno, a shape that is repeated in the hillside above, where the river turns back westward to flow rather hastily through Florence and into its more direct, headlong rush to Pisa and the Tyrrhenian Sea.

The neat, white, rounded headstones of the American Cemetery, in their military rows on the flat and always green lawn—even lately, during the worst drought in recent memory—often make me more aware of my fellow commuters. Mainly they are the provincial generation of the Valdarno of the eighties and nineties heading toward vocational high schools or the University of Florence. Cell phones in hand, they beep out messages to their boyfriends and girlfriends or highlight class notes in fluorescent green, yellow, or orange in preparation for their exams. They, like most of my own American students, are the first generation no longer connected orally to the war over fascism.

Since the train tracks run just beneath the hillsides of the ridge that follows the river's course, the stations on this line sit on the high ground, at the outer edge of the towns built along the river. And since Napoleon outlawed the tradition of burying the Christian dead in or around the parish churches of Italy, the Le Sieci station is flanked on the one side by the town and the river below it and on the other by a walled and gated cemetery cut into the hillside overlooking both. This modern construction sits on the slope of the ridge, above its parking lot, like a sterile little city of its own. Once, I remember, a cell phone–carrying young woman, annoyed by the train's lateness and complaining vociferously throughout the journey, added this fact to her series of lamentations: "*Il cimitero*," she observed, looking out the window sarcastically, "*che allegria!*" Her contempt for her dead countrymen and women's presence, begrudging them even this cement tenement where they are stacked six or seven high — although it was perhaps natural for someone so young and already annoyed by the passage of time — saddened me all the same.

Although he flew mostly over atolls in the South Seas and dropped bombs on whatever looked suspicious from a military standpoint, I sometimes think that my own father could easily have ended up in the American Cemetery and that I might not be on this train at all; that, in some imaginary scenario, I too could be buried down there with my father's contemporaries. I might well have been left unborn; awash in the wake of MacArthur's triumphant return, part of a briny skeleton in a Corsair, always an unrealized part of my father, and neither of us would ever have known my mother. Or perhaps obliterated, incinerated against a volcanic island or instantaneously set aflame in the air by a burp gun over Korea where my father also flew 108 missions in defense of the American way of life in a country of rice paddies and kimchee. He did all this before ever meeting my mother, before I was conceived.

One summer I shared an apartment in a medieval fortification outside of Siena with a Korean sculptor and his family—he had come to Italy to learn to work in marble and was taking language courses at the school for foreigners in Siena before moving on to Massa Carrara for an intensive workshop in rock carving. Curious to see his reaction, I told him that my father had fought in the Korean War. Tears welled up in his eyes, and he told me to thank my father for all that he had done for a free Korea. Although the sculptor knew only a few words of either English or Italian, and we were never really able to communicate, he and his family always treated me with an exaggerated respect bordering on reverence.

This oddly reminds me of the time that one of my students asked me which side Italy had been on in World War II. Of course it depends upon what you mean by Italy and who you ask. I imagine that most of my students don't know that fascism is an Italian word. My wife's grandfathers might well have killed my own father had he been Ethiopian or the invading Fifth Army—as I assume the soldiers in the American Cemetery were. Although neither of them seems to have spoken much about the war once it was over, one of my wife's grandfathers was apparently reduced to drinking his own urine and eating his company's donkey in the North African desert—a real trauma for a member of one of the most culinary of nationalities—and I hear them now on their cell phones telling their mammas what they had for lunch today and when they'll be getting home for dinner. My wife's other grandfather was deported to a Nazi work camp in Germany. He apparently walked most of the way back to the Mugello and was given up for dead by his family long before arriving home. He carried back a deluxe radio from the ruins of the Third Reich that now sits in my mother-in-law's livingroom, a family heirloom.

Growing up, I myself was faced with the dualistic knowledge that my father was something of a war hero and the nightly vision on the TV news of protesters spitting on soldiers either heading to or returning home from Vietnam. I can still hear them chanting "Hell no—we won't go!" and see that naked, napalm-scarred little girl running toward the *Life* magazine photographer whose photo made the "Year In Pictures" number, which I religiously saved as a collector's item. I played war like everybody else, and I don't remember having any particular opinions about it, despite the nightly news. Real wars were too far away in either space or time to really have any effect on me. I remember the kids on the school bus chanting "Nixon!" and "McGovern!" back and forth depending on for whom their fathers were voting. I went down to campaign headquarters and got a big Nixon poster and a bunch of stickers and had fun sticking the adhesives to the poster and hanging it up in my room. This advertisement/shrine was still hanging there during the Watergate scandal, and it became the emblem of my growing political awareness, my social conscience, the consciousness of how comforting powerlessness is, as I grew into high school age.

I remember my father mentioning, out of conscience, that he could probably get me into West Point if I wanted to go there instead of the dinky state university where I had planned to go to study business administration and English literature. Of course he knew that I would reject the proposal, but he didn't want me to realize later that it had been a possibility and complain that he had never brought it up. Although not much of a baseball fan, a convinced Republican, and something of a racist, my father is, perversely, a very good guy. Sometimes I wonder if I'm not rather his opposite, an a-moral son of a bitch with all of the correct political views.

As is probably already obvious from the observations and style of this text, my own life is so interior as to be practically nonexistent. I do not believe that any action I will ever take in the world will be historically significant in any way other than statistically. Nor does this bother me. I will second James Joyce and declare, in this, my forty-first year of existence, that history is a nightmare from which I am trying to awake. Obviously this text belies my reliance on history as the false mother that shapes us all, as the womb against which we struggle to be born as individuals, the forgetting of which is both tragic and liberating.

Fairly recently I discovered that the patriarchal side of my family is Pennsylvania Dutch and has been in the United States since colonial days. I had a great-great-great grandfather who fought in the Revolutionary War under General George Washington at the battle of Princeton. This is amusing in a couple of ways. Obviously, because the battle happened in a town now so much more famous for its university, and since I am a university administrator, it strikes me as ironic. Also I now have a historical and biological model of a rebellious nature—which, should I decide coincides with my present self, would be so interior as to be absolutely a-historical and, in the eyes of many, perhaps hypocritical. Did I feel differently about myself before I knew of my ancestor's pseudo-rebellious and probably meager military exploit? Of course. From now on, for the rest of my life, I will in some small sense always be the progeny of a revolutionary or an anti-imperialist race, even if, like most people, my ancestors only really fought for economic and not physical or moral freedom, as the patriots would prefer to figure it.

Ah, freedom, that most misused and misunderstood of words. The word that seems to send every proud soldier to their marble white-on-green manicured cemetery or bloody incineration, their name on an endless black marble monument in Washington, DC, or the few local names on the fading white World War I plaques that adorn the walls of the parish churches of Italy. The word that launched a thousand ships for Troy, the very launching of which cost Iphigenia her life, her throat slit on an altar like a lamb, or that naked Vietnamese girl crying and running from a rain of burning gasoline. Annually now I read and teach Virgil's *Aeneid*, a text that simultaneously glorifies and bemoans the sacrifices made to war, to the building of an empire, or to seeing one's historical destiny through to its end. We are allowed to speak for these victims because we are the children of the survivors of wars. My own son is once again the legacy of all of the soldiers who survived these many wars, whether spit on or paraded, vociferous or silently traumatized, winner or loser, drunk or sober, both American and Italian.

Passing by the American Cemetery today, I have the inevitable feeling that it is flowing outside of its manicured hedges and into the streets. My fellow commuters continue on with their family and school concerns—they neither chant the names of presidential candidates nor seem overly concerned that their country is run by a political party that exploits soccer slogans and private TV stations for its popularity. The newspapers are full of programmatically random acts of violence that seem to prove that war is really all about outmaneuvering death on a daily basis; that it is more about survival than liberation.

The American Cemetery seems to have a new, larger mission today; a global mission that alternately offers a helping hand or a bayonet point to the economically oppressed, whichever is most expedient. It's opening up its gates now to include a whole new world of struggle and sacrifice in the name of economic freedom. In its white-on-green order, its forgotten commemoration of the war for and against fascism, the rubble is continually coming down around our heads or igniting buses in public streets like firecrackers on the Fourth of July. Or just bombs, always bombs, coming down impersonally from above. Quite suddenly, surprisingly, I have a silent and peaceful—although terrifying—sensation that we're all jumping from the Twin Towers to avoid the flames inside of our own consciences, floating out into space in an exhilarating newsreel image of a weightless future.

11/26/2003
S. Francesco

SPARAGMOS

The perfume vats have slopped over,
flooding the streets of Florence with sweet
stink, and there's nothing I can do about it.

We don't get paid a living wage
for what we do, her boyfriend
doesn't do her when she needs doing,

and there's nothing I can do
but sit and listen. There's nothing
to be done when the cars keep coming

and the brakes on my bike
don't work, and the bank steals your world
away 9.50 € at a time — month in

and month out. And there's no point
in touching the computer screen; you're
two months out of touch, asking

for Gypsy change, wishing you were
Penny Rimbaud with a country
retreat safe enough for an anarchist

convention. And Max is dead,
a knife in his gut on the bed
where he let strangers fuck him

so as not to feel so alone
when strangers fucked him, alone
in the slow dismemberment that Psyche

,the goddess, never could have predicted,
her womb the center of an archaic worldview
Christ knew nothing about.

And your resurrection? Will it pay
these bills? Will it wash these windows
we look through? Will it make us whole

or wholesale?

       4/10/2011
       Florence

EUPHORIA

I

New white electric sneakers, a row of lights in the rubber soles, saw-teeth scraping the blacktop at every step, fingernails down the blackboard, baby crying in the next room, like you left your cell phone somewhere strange, forgot to take your Lithium—and it's getting dark.

I, on the other hand, feel good right now. No dead-end hysteria today; no, siree. They let me up out of the airless tank today, and I don't care that nothing means anything anymore, that nothing means anything sometimes, or even that something doesn't always mean anything later on and that we'll all be dead in a hundred years anyway—all new people! Imagine that—or that they just elected that crook president again. They're all crooks anyway so who cares; it might as well be the crook we're used to rather than a crook we might trust.

Skeletons are smiling today.

These are the days during which I enjoy peeping through the creaking door and mentally groping the passerby.

Today it's armoire-changing weather. The Americans are already bra-less, tank-topped, their layered stomachs protruding—belly-button rings and all—over the brims of their low-waisted jeans. Flip-flops, dirty blond hair, stubble, sunburns, and cow eyes; not exactly stupid, but ominously intent on sticking their muzzles into the short grass, endlessly still and green: Florence's infinitely chewable cultural fodder.

The natives, however, are all winter-zipped up to their throats (invisible steel poles still firmly fixed, from their assholes up through their spines to their turbaned heads) and pivoting their characteristically disapproving sneers from right to left and left to right as they exit their individual voting booths. No tan lines. Yet.

A half a billion cell phones connect to the other half a billion cell phones in a bitter exchange of pleasantries: "*Dove sei?*" and "*hai mangiato?*" Yes! Fried baby entrails with parsley and saccharine—doctor's orders, I'm trying to cut down on starch and cholesterol.

The war is over! Long live MacDonald's!

Of course there are the cars of Italy; old news, devastation, the collective expression of my own suicidal tenancies. The moment in which going back to smoking almost seems like a good idea comes and goes.

Even this city, "where the almighty willed that my lady should live,"[*] looks like potential cow cud today, endless waving fields of consumability on sale, snot dripping from a loose tendril or two. The sun comes and goes—a Doors LP cover to a London fog in a global something or other salad—and I'm euphorically alone on my park bench for the first time in eighteen years.

I'm attached to life today, in the trenches with Ungaretti—and the war's over. (*Evviva il cellulare!*) This is just mopping up operations, washing the dog shit from the sidewalks of Florence, fertilizing the Uffizi for the cows to come (despite the cost) this summer.

II

This, however, is the last academic IRT, freezing cold in early June, drunk and hard, alone and eerily alone because "Love is all around why don't you take it."[*] I'm feeling the contours of the gray matter tonight, sensuous brain-flesh touched first by the gaze and then the squishy fingers of subway lovers, no pain despite the exposed sinews of pink and gray—the brain never bleeds like it should. New York City is always like this, inside out, talking to you in the street, pushing you out of the way, smiling at you, ignoring you, half dressed for the summer heat and the dampness of its own tenuous existence, opening you again and again to all

---

[*] Dante Alighieri, *Vita Nova*.
[*] *Mary Tyler Moore Show* theme song.

desires and then plunking you down sweating and cold in a refrigerated subway car.

From island to island, coast to coast, death, blight, and destruction incorporated of Saskatchewan, Ontario, in the orange and black television screen— oak-wise from Oaktown a home is a home would smell as sweet would be a place if I were an I but this I is everyperson on this train in euphoric in-between Saturday night subway riding martini-smeared sensuality.

In-between again, like all good second acts.

III

And now I know that home—there is no home— desire—there is no desire—and that the heart is where the mind hangs its hat.

It appears that the summer has finally revealed what could only have been dreamt of in the spring: that the spaces through which I was destined to pass would be as empty as the heart to which I had for so long pledged my faith. I knew then that the boobs would come out for the summer, and they have, that the Florentines would change their armor and armoires and they have; that the tourists, my fellow Americans, would come and go home again, chewing this town up like pizza and cannoli in the process, and that all of my prophesies have come to pass.

New York is alone now, hot and cold and humid, Eighth Avenue has lost its voice, and smoky Oakland swelters while the rest of California burns dry and golden in the sun.

Between *veltro* and *veltro*, I turn back to these pages for consolation and advice, and the page mirrors my spaces perfectly, my expectations of both disaster and comfort, my loneliness, my solitude, my understanding and my now hopeful future—and this Cassandra can still see how it will be: it's going to be a long, cold winter.

BETTI BLU'S MORTGAGE

Winter streets and frozen
fountains how easy
to forgive oneself the chill

leaves burning on the plain
'neath Orvieto. Your eyes
the same skewed colors as

my own, turned down
sterile, stern, on
our child in disapproval.

And now these giggling girls
you forgot yourself in
putrid memories, this train

sunk in soggy ponds
and the bloody chamber
of Bluebeard's secret room

where you walled us all up.

2/17/2009
Florence-Rome, in transit

BENEATH THE ONE AND ONLY SUN
IN A PLACE CALLED TUSCANY

"During a dry season the clods are bigger and more chunky next to that seared field of dead sunflowers," the Irish tourist imagines from his seat on the bus winding its way uphill to Volterra from Colle Val d'Elsa. He's done it a million times, certain as he is of the ubiquitous nature of his imagination's capacity to turn all of his observations into a single, viable reality. "In California, in 'the golden state,'" he muses, "the earth sighs gently and nestles itself comfortably inside the color of the sun, but this summer the Tuscan landscape is screaming through a washed-out and bone-bleached beige. And County Cork," he laughs at the indicative contradiction, "is always an emerald green."

"How hard it is to catch a farmer out in the summer sun; 'though it can only be through their piss and vinegar that these vineyards remain verdant at all. Even the sere olive trees would cry out if not for their centuries-old exhaustion," he observes.

"I cried for you too, Molly, when they threw the curtains open, and the sun once again earned its epithet, 'pitiless.' Or perhaps more for me'self."

Power lines are newly drooping over dust-storm tractors up around the bend. "Mad dogs and Englishmen." The blue regional busses hump, slug-like, about the low-lying hills of *"umile Italia,"* for intrepid tourists and auto-less locals. "Here a villa, there a villa (in which the inbred aristocracy toast their depravity in the form of antique bric-a-brac).

"I should massage that lump.

"Giacomo Joyce rather knew what he was talkin' about, don'tcha know.

"At last the Britons have raised the flag of empire above Bald Mountain (despite so many Yankee tourists), colonizing the Bristles and chaining their children to the doubly-bound right to exercise a reasonable freedom of religion (excepting all of that darky mucky-muck of course). But where is the moon if the sun never sets on their empire? Lost, perhaps, in a cloud of soldier-raised marching dust? Empirically sterile.

"Me thoughts are well able to destroy such conquests considerably faster than any Mayan calendar, sprat and lean replacing the festering finger of ol' Saint Bartholomew (or even the venerable Thomas) in churches up and down the many islands that merely imitate Eire *cum* Hibernium.

"I pointed it at ya, Molly, all night long, but the daylight could never come that would betray it to these swarthy heathen Neapolitan jackanapes.

"The Etruscan acropolis high atop Renaissance Vola'erre turns out to be," according to another Gaelic interpretive leap, "a natural rock formation subject to the nostalgic fantasies of an archeologist, a certain 'Simon,' who, despising Christian hypocrisy, created a mythic history involving a race of soldiers he calls 'Romans' and an even wilder and considerably less distinct tribe known as 'Etruscans,' who imported Neapolitan artisans here in order to decorate the first ever holy building in the Etrurian wine-tasting region."

Rocks are hard — to read — after all.

Someone is chopping lumber up here: "Well, if you've got wood... As if there could ever be another winter after such a painstakingly hot sacking of the region with blinding sunlight and arid palms. (Even the grapes look peaked.) Land-locked pirates moan lowly at intervals — or is it merely motocross?" Later, the tolling of the lonely church bell fails to disturb the chattering of the cicadas.

Amused, bemused by his own antics, as always, he entices the hornets' nest to re-invention: "*Destati, o voce d'Italia! L'afa non annaffia le farfalle fetenti. Tee-hee.*"

Then, in the duomo ...

"The characteristic gesture continues to both comfort and annoy. Perhaps that's why the West once tired of art as it did away with a certain amount of human suffering and abuse. Ends and means intertween without much trouble, don'tcha know. In order to yell it's best to have something to shout about — or *shite abite*, as the cockney says. Too much utopia is not good for the artist or the actor — Satan is always a more compelling character than any kitschy icon. (I will invoke neither.) White and green marble teeth ruminate upon Etruria's truce with Christianity in any Episcopal seat worth its salt."

The afternoon wind blows in off of the sea, rolls on up the hill, and the few resurrected columns of the Roman amphitheater defy it by remaining erect.

"Perhaps I should allow the Romans to exist if only as a model for the institutional barbarity their empire has begotten in a million other cultures' bellies. Clean and pressed uniforms and enough colorful rows of expressionless soldiery were always capable of drowning out the screams of the gratefully repressed in a sea of white supremacy. We abolished slavery, once, with the triumph of Christianity in Europe, but forgot about the theatre, let books slip from our fingers, and stopped teaching our children how to read — such was our new material wellbeing. Utopia at the cost of boredom. Without Nazis or Klingons …

"Vola'erre's walls and gates will not enclose me tonight. Once again I'll be on me own. And no 'Waltzing Matilda' either."

8/23/2012
Volterra

FLORENCE

Florence,
Like a lover, spread
before me, unrelentingly
itself, indifferent to me
and all my bitter euphoria.

Florence,
in the rain, clouds seeded
with desire spent, and desire
regained and that sad old fucker
,full in the sky, over my shoulder
        followed me home

— then, when the smoke cleared —

An habitué of years
of lonely Florentine nights;
I pissed on the Fortezza,
walked along the Mugnone
,invisible as Calandrino,
        — no heliotrope in *my* pockets —
writing text messages as your train
lurched toward the Apennines, lurched toward the
Alps

and I found your scent
        in my room:
It was like coming
        face to face
with my own ghost.

I named her Florence.

        12/14/2008
        Florence

CAMELS AND WATER

Glanced at through the grime-bespattered window of the train, that suburb of Perugia, San Giovanni, glared back at the two American travelers flat and square in all of its defensive aplomb. The slick and predictable cement new town at the bottom of the hill presented itself as a series of disconnected but straight lines leading directly to the lives of its high-rise dwellers. The couple that saw these buildings lined up in front of the derelict station from the windows of the Chiusi train — without looking directly at them, or even noting them particularly — were making their escape from Florence, seeking an asylum of sorts in the obliquely scenic hill towns of Umbria. Assisi for a start, as the naked merchant meditative saint linked them at their point of origin: for they had met in San Francisco, California, some twenty years before.

The ridge of mountains running alongside of the train's southeastern trajectory were *spoglie*, naked stone mostly, and seemed to be leading them toward a springtime sun that Florence had not yet anticipated that year. Nakedness had already struck her as a keynote to their trip, to their nascent coupledom, the lack of plaster covering the rocky buildings of the hill towns, his way of expressing desire by stripping for her, his ugly honesty in the face of her coy tact. The train balances them on its straight tracks between the two continents. The Hotel Fortezza gives them, finally, some privacy, and they get down to the business of middle age: taking naps and arranging their life together around meal times.

"Florence is the beach that I keep washing up on to when my various ships go down. But survival is a dirty business, a booby prize at best, and little consolation — more like an endless series of appointments to keep. And I'm usually late."

She sleeps through his silent, imaginary speeches with jet lag, dreaming of foghorns, of San Francisco-grey skies, of other people's children, and the gibberish of Italian voices in her head: ugly, complaining Florentine voices.

"Why is everyone here so angry?" she asks.

An old woman sitting in the first springtime sun outside of her home in Assisi tells them that the town is effectively moribund, that what had struck the travelers as Mediterranean calm was rather the deadly cold of the tenacious winter just now passing, an absence of heat, of the sun and its light, the emptiness of so many centuries lived inside the socialized pink stone of the mountainside. The city was not so clean, as they had surmised, because of its municipal efficiency, but because no one had been there all winter long to soil its Subasian limestone streets. "There is not even a supermarket here." Life was, apparently, elsewhere — as they had already noted in the city's strangely tasteless food.

Just as the saint's identity constructs itself around the story of his or her martyrdom, so Assisi goes on quietly in meditation of its losses—and of the things that it had never had to endure. Flying in the face of all this history—and the current economic crisis—Francis' renunciation of commerce had begun to lose its power. "Perhaps he was more of an exhibitionist than a protester, preferring to display his natural endowments over the baubles of his bourgeois clothes and finery in the public square. Maybe he was seeking a radical rearrangement of the rules of status—my God, do you remember San Gimignano and all those towers?

"Even Clair might have achieved a new, as yet unthought-of beauty with her locks shorn in the piazza, by laying down the symbol of her vanity. It seems like we always associate bald women with dishonor. Like in *For Whom the Bell Tolls*, or the images of the women in Nazi concentration camps, standing in the snow in their striped pajamas, or their naked and frozen bodies lying in heaps on the ground. Baldness, even nakedness, becomes the mark of the victim, of the shame of being singled out for martyrdom—of being so special.

"Images like these create a new kind of beauty too, become unborn fetishes, announce new unthought-of pleasures that only strike the viewer when they are seen for the first time." He's thinking of the cover of Patti Smith's *Easter* as he says this, a certain silly photo of a woman on a unicycle glimpsed in a *Playboy* magazine when he was an adolescent, a freckled redhead sunbathing in a nudist magazine hidden in his parents' bedroom.

Comments like these belie their voyeuristic culture, their Facebook reunion after twenty years of the day-to-day grind with nearer relations. It's now more likely than ever that they should fall in love, like the knights and grand dames of old, by reputation alone, across oceans and between continents — even though such happenings are more properly a convention of triangular Medieval romance narratives. Perhaps the population of Assisi had been sucked through cyberspace and into a new world of personal subjectivity, leaving the town's cold, pink streets clear of traffic for our casual tourists.

Yet often the pain of so much loss, of time and its scythe, of an odd emptiness, felt real and palpable in Assisi — between the museums, the restaurants and the coffee bars, despite all of one's strategies of escape, reconciliation, and the advertising.

Separation, isolation, spending the winter on the side of a mountain in a largely uninhabited Medieval hill-town, the lack of privacy or understanding of his Florentine landlords, like the man who, emerging from the water after a shipwreck, turns back to survey the deep sea from which he has escaped. Florence and its florid nonbeing was always there over his shoulder to piss him off, to throw his own mediocrity and complicity in all of its bourgeois architecture back at him. Assisi, on the other hand, caressed them coolly, even if its fingers were bony winter branches with unsprouted buds for knuckles. Spring would indeed come, the midday sun promised, even if the wind was still busy blowing March up and down the peninsula like a seesaw, exacerbating both his and her allergies.

"No, I didn't dream of anything, but I could hear myself sleeping, hear myself making funny noises." Her face is sleep-flushed, puffy-red, and her eyes shine and smile.

"Why did we never make noise at night when we were young?"

"I was paralyzed: I could hear myself sleeping but couldn't wake myself up."

"Jet-lag."

She doesn't remember that he once slept on the floor of her bedroom in San Francisco. Walking her home after a rock show somewhere, too tired or drunk to make it back to his place.

"I seem to remember you wearing little boy pajamas."

"And I made you sleep on the floor?"

"You must have been in love with someone else at the time."

She photographs him in the streets, in the castle, as she had photographed him and his son in Florence and Lucca. She frames the basilica, the castle, the Villa Fidelia, Spello, and Assisi, abstracting their buildings and streets once and for all. Walking the night-dark cobblestone streets after dinner, they find themselves alone on the highest road in town, in a kind of shadow-land between the medieval castle above and the main square below. When the streetlights dwindle, leaving the road a blank field of darkness before them, she is terrified—and yet there is nowhere else she would rather be. Reluctantly, they descend back to the town's single thoroughfare, only to have to climb back up again further along to get back to their hotel.

"I remember lying on the hardwood floor, looking upside-down at the full moon outside of the bay window."

"I hope I gave you a pillow at least."

He takes some consolation from the asymmetry of the medieval buildings, the obviously ad hoc way in which the Etruscan blocks have formed the bases for the Roman walls, and the Roman walls providing the rubble used to build the medieval houses, which had then been covered over with the plaster veneer of Renaissance symmetry. "'The lid on the garbage,' as Adorno said of culture," he says. Then the Gothic biform windows give way to the post and lintel, crooked narrow stairways to palatial Renaissance grandeur, and finally the Baroque curve—which had passed Umbria by in favor of Rome and Naples. Only the dry, parking-garage-based post-war apartment complexes along the freeway and train tracks on the Umbrian plain (following alongside the ancient Via Flaminia without actually touching it) link the orphaned cities of the region—Assisi, Spello, Gubbio, Todi, and Perugia—only they have escaped imitation, snug in their "*zone Industriali*." That rebellion, un-reclaiming the farmland of the floodplain with inconsequential architecture, is almost alarming in its banality.

Such a reconstruction of Italy is indicative, he thinks, of his ex-wife's slash-and-burn mentality and is greatly to be feared should it infect his son. How he himself has managed to escape such inborn inconsequentiality and its complementary cultural nihilism in a similarly sanitized California suburb is still something of a mystery. He seeks the origins of his love of words, of history, of human imagination and ingenuity, of the decaying past and all of its intricacies, whenever possible, in the castles and tombs of Italy's medieval and ancient past. He even tries to sound out his companion on such matters, but she escapes him in daydreams and photographs, telling him that she has worked for architects who designed prisons while they stand on the back porch of St. Francis' basilica, between its two levels, beside the gift shop.

"I was thinking about the Franciscans who built the missions in California, like Mission Dolores. I remember reading that they tried to get the Indians to race, because the monks, being Europeans, thought that the Indians were lazy. They had to beat the Indians to get them to race against each other. Since Indians only ever ran when they were hunting, and since they hunted in groups, they couldn't understand why it was so important to the monks that one of them should run faster than all of the others, such a thing just didn't make any sense to them."

She travels a great deal and the bare statement of it, of almost all of the things that she tells him, is enough. The calm narrative voice of a True Crime TV station lulls her to sleep at night in San Francisco just as he listens to recordings of the radio dramas of the 1940s in order to escape having to look at a world made up of so many moving images as he drifts away from it and into sleep in his apartment in Florence.

They huddle close together in the hotel room bed, linger in the photo-worthy streets and piazzas, between so much stone that it prompts him to pause and to muse on the toughness of the Etruscan character.

"Wood surely has softened us from our earliest days."

Outside of Spello, a smaller, less-traveled Umbrian hill-town, they stalk the Villa Fidelia and the minor genius of an overenthusiastic decorative artist who has made the quaint and theatrical little villa tourist worthy. The cypresses in its decorative gardens lay in wait for them to scratch at their eyes and open, with sneezes, the floodgates of slippery hot phlegm in their noses. All is quiet and sullen in the wisteria-covered byways of the gardens and in the shortbread-colored rooms of the villa, restored but aloof, out of season. Imagining themselves to be Hansel and Gretel, they await the blind old witch—but they are not allowed into the villa's kitchen. Another pair of tourists eventually wanders into the well-kept grounds; they stare at each other with diffidence, each couple guarding their solitude.

The people that they meet in the town seem to welcome them and their coming, hailing this announcement of the tourist season, the first unfamiliar faces of the new year, veterans of the wars—neither backpackers, religious pilgrims, nor refugees—strangely together after so many other voyages. It has been a long lonely winter, apparently, for all concerned. He asks her if they can revisit the Basilica of Saint Francis on their last day in Assisi, and it may be that its two separate but indivisible structural and temporal levels will provide them with a model—barring more earthquakes either here or in Northern California.

"I was studying here during the earthquake of '89. Didn't you write to me back then? I used to have all of the letters of my old San Francisco friends telling me where they were when it happened, what they were doing, and what it was like afterwards—no power or lights and the fires in the Marina burning through the night."

"I do remember writing to you back then. Then we fell out of touch."

She had still been working at Green Apple—had been practically buried alive under the books when the shelves had toppled down all around her.

"I'm having a problem with the continuum still. I want to tell everyone I meet that I have an Italian child, that I am a resident of this country, of this here and now, a tourist by chance and not by vocation."

"I'm comfortable," she says, perhaps meaning only in her chair outside of the café, the warm afternoon waning all around the terrace, the tasty flute of prosecco before her on the tablecloth that's clipped to the table against the wind. She never speaks of the novelty of their situation, their having known each other twenty years before, his now apparently permanent residence in this foreign country, nor the sporadic nature of their crepuscular romance.

As they look off across the main square and its tentative re-managing of the Roman forum beneath, the future wavers before them like a mirage that is perhaps, if they have enough camels and water, obtainable. Then again, perhaps the image would vanish when her visit ended and she returned to Francis' other city, leaving him alone once again in the turmoil of his private gauntlet against the backdrop of the daily round of lessons and Florentine scowls. Then she leans across the table, smiling, and kisses him.

Later, at Peretola, Florence's Mickey Mouse airport, they make her take, humiliatingly, a bus across the tarmac to her tiny connecting flight's airplane. Even so, he cannot resist saying, just before she steps through the metal detector, "We'll always have Assisi."

3/2009
Assisi & Florence

ZWARIOWANY KAPELUSZNIK

(For Jeff and Karolina — but also for Magdalena, Chris, and Anna)

"When you live in a place, you must eat the bread of its people." — Jeff Gburek

Will the Mad Hatnik ever relinquish his hoary grip on our hearts? He is a fickle fiend who desires his own undoing above all other enterprises. He met the devil at the crossroads — Zürich, by chance, when his flights were rerouted — and had no need to sell his soul, having recognized in himself his own only single double indemnity policy's sole beneficiary.

Hitchhiking back to Algeria, by way of Abernathy, he consoles himself with erotic daydreams and vodka suppositories. However, even in this he is not alone: for Alhambra Akhmatova, his accomplice, has laid the road bare by vanishing again and again into imaginary existence. The very trees tremble at the power of the misadventures that they silently vow never to effectively have.

And lies? He could tell nothing else, not even time, and yet his cell phone bloomed yellow and blue in the sun through cracks that led, all too predictably, to the underworld.

Yet suicide might actually be a way, so say I (and James Hogg), of rooting out the devil's truffle. However—no, not "but," anything but "but"—however, descent was unnecessary for *this*, our own land, turned out to be that of the dead—a salvific portal to all places, a Slavonic city of the central plain, so necessary to the nomads of the steppes and the rioters of '56, a place of heartening renewal, where union is celebrated from the bottom of a beer glass up: where love cannot matter and, devoid of matter, is ever so lovely.

Craven indeed is that helpless double who cannot look himself in the eye, buy at least half of his own soul, ring his imaginary lady's finger, smile at the camera, doff his hat, and save his own soul through the suicide of a lady's man.

6/21/2010
Poznan-Florence, in transit

but what if words fall short?
what if, unaffected, the world
and our terse faces
                    keep on falling

through days, down streets
of insidious intent, on the road
and "bent to it"
                    as the prosist says?

Americans: on the way
to all our metaphysical nowheres —

the film plays at six, eight, and ten
            (two and four on Saturdays and Sundays)
we'll sit through it w/out speaking

the abyss doesn't bother me
                    anymore

                    i can use it
                    to understand.

9/30/1994
NYC

AFTERWORD

This compilation of short stories, poems, prose experiments, and prose poems is, for me, a literary framing of a few of the many occasional texts culled from the notebooks that I have filled with writing over the years; it represents a kind of selective diary of narratives, observations, and tonal meditations upon this author's fascination with place—both in terms of a physical landscape, an imagined geography, as well as a conceptual space either of belonging or otherness, a home or a strange place that one visits for whatever reasons: curiosity, escape, or for that measuring of the self that unfamiliar places seem to invite—even provoke.

As the title of the collection suggests, perhaps the best way to access the various narrators' experiences recounted herein, to define their singular lack of a stable personality or literary method, is to think of each text as a sojourner, a voice who enters, inhabits briefly, and then, for one reason or another, abandons each place in favor of the next. A dear friend once remarked that, like a bird, I tend to settle into other people's nests, hatch myself there, and then fly off toward some distant horizon. It remains for the reader to decide if it is I who have left my mark on these many places, mostly cities, by inscribing their names and some words about them into the notebooks that have fed this collection or vice versa.

Taken together, the disparate texts that make up *Sojourner* can be read as the fictionalized and poetic chronicle of my wandering years, which began in 1986 when, at the tender age of twenty-four, I left San Francisco for Europe planning never to return, and which have more or less continued up to the present day. I have lived these, my adult years, at first willfully, later accidentally, as a transitory sojourner, experiencing first several European capitals as a traveler, then Florence and New York City as an itinerant student, and finally some ten years in a little piss-trough of a town outside of Florence called San Francesco as a teacher, a husband, and a father.

During my decade in San Francesco I used to joke that my autobiography would be called *From San Francisco to San Francesco*, but my ex-wife had other plans. Which brings me to what putting these texts together has taught me is the overriding theme of my writing (and I suppose my life as well): solitude and companionship, otherness and familiarity, both between people as well as with places — a situation that constructs, in these texts, the themes of chance encounters, identity, self-destruction, escape and dreams, compromise, resurrection or transformation, desire, and, of course, traveling. We fly, "like a demon, from station to station," as David Bowie sings.

I write this afterword from a rented room back in Florence, Italy, during my fifth sojourn in this city. I have a four-year lease, with an option for another four, which I might see out or which I might break any day in favor of a room in Naples, Oakland, Rome, New York City, or anywhere else they will have me. Just as the day I left San Francisco some twenty-six years ago, with three thousand dollars in travelers' checks and a one-way ticket to Brussels in my pocket, the world remains my oyster.

I hear that, with a little Vernaccia, they slide down pretty smoothly.

11/19/2012
Florence

Earlier versions of "Sojourner" and "The American Cemetery" first appeared in Jill Stauffer's *H2SO4* magazine, in issue number thirteen (Summer/Autumn 2000) and issue number nineteen (Autumn/Winter 2004), respectively.

An earlier version of "Romance (an Episodic Narrative)" first appeared in issue #1 (Winter 2009) of Frank Andrick's *WTF* magazine under the title "A Poem About Commuting on the *Ferrovia Italiana*."

Special thanks are due to both of these fine editors.

My heartfelt thanks also go out to Jeff Gburek, Kathleen Nichols, and to Marc Gilson, whose editing suggestions have made this book much better than it might have been otherwise, and especially to Debra A. Zeller for invaluable moral support and fantastic photos and cover design.